AND MAYBE NOT

Marjorie Campbell

∞INFINITY
PUBLISHING

Fictional Work
Copyright © 2013 by Marjorie Ann Campbell
Cover Photo by Marjorie Campbell
Author's Photo by Stuart Garfield

ISBN 978-0-7414-9949-3

Printed in the United States of America

Published December 2013

INFINITY PUBLISHING
1094 New DeHaven Street, Suite 100
West Conshohocken, PA 19428-2713
Toll-free (877) BUY BOOK
Local Phone (610) 941-9999
Fax (610) 941-9959
Info@buybooksontheweb.com
www.buybooksontheweb.com

Dedicated to the memory of
Marjorie Rourke Campbell and
Raphael Joseph Campbell
Who were parents extraordinaire

"…And other strains of woe,
which now seem woe,
Compared with the loss of thee
will not seem so."

—William Shakespeare, *Sonnet Number 90*

CHAPTER

1977

This couldn't be true. He couldn't be doing this. But his hands tightened on her throat, and she quickly realized that he was serious. Dead serious. His face, contorted with rage, was almost unrecognizable. The pressure on her throat was becoming unbearable and the fingernails that she had planted in the backs of his hands were having no effect. It took all of her strength to keep trying to suck air into her burning lungs and her vision was dimming.

She calmly realized that she had drifted above her body, and was looking down on it and her killer. She heard unfamiliar, but beautiful music, and slowly felt that she had become one with a beautiful golden light. A warm hand slipped into hers and a gentle, loving voice said, "Welcome home."

CHAPTER

Port Locke, Massachusetts

"The Commonwealth of Massachusetts commands your appearance," I read aloud from the official-looking document that had arrived in the morning mail.

"Commands?" I huffed, addressing my friend Cass, who was kneeling against the back of my couch applying mascara to about a hundred images of her eyelashes reflected in my infinity mirror.

"I don't think I care for the Commonwealth's tone in this communication," I continued, waving the paper in her direction.

Cass snorted. "Command this…throw it out."

"I don't know. This is, after all, my second deewee this year and I don't care to spend the summer playing shortstop for the Framingham women's prison's softball team."

"Of course not," Cass agreed. "If they don't let you pitch, don't play." Then, with one of her customary whip-lashing segues, announced, "I'm ready," and headed for the front door of my condo.

I demurred. "I really think I may have to do the right thing here and give it up."

Cass stopped short and turned around. "Drinking?" she asked in a voice that was several octaves higher than normal.

I laughed. "Don't be stupid. Driving."

I balled up the summons and threw it to Phineas, my chinchilla Persian Cat/Person, who caught it in his two front double paws and threw it on the floor with exactly the same disdain that Cass had expressed.

**

CHAPTER

Bamberg, Germany 1629

Like her mother and grandmother, Anke Johannes was a healer. She grew herbs for the creation of her potions, the recipes for which had been passed through mother to daughter for generations. She relieved pain and cured illnesses. The striking blonde wise woman was well-known in her village of Greisling and the surrounding hamlets. She lived with her son on a small but fertile farm and made a good living from it. She sometimes accepted fees for her services as a wise woman, but never demanded payment from anyone.

In the winter of 1629, even she had been confounded by a strange fever that had beset the area. She could find no explanation or cure for the illness as it took the lives of one child after another. She did her best to find the right elixir, but failed.

Late one night, a Greisling man, inconsolable after losing two children to the mysterious illness, stood outside of her house and screamed, "Your child lives while mine are gone. *Witch!*"

Church and government were always pleased to relieve a female healer of the position. Important things like medicine should be left to men and God, preferably in that order. Anke was considered *named* by the grieving father and an arrest warrant was issued. Additionally, the Church could make far better use of the nice little farm.

**

CHAPTER

Port Locke, Massachusetts

I live in a condo on Clock Tower Wharf in a seaside town just north of Boston. The building is within crawling distance of six bars. Having been twice bagged on deewees (Driving While Impaired), I did the responsible thing and gave my Impala convertible to my brother Doc, who is an impoverished professional student -- with the understanding that he and the car would be my transportation providers as required.

Clock Tower Wharf is so named for being a wharf that extends seaward from a wooden clock tower that was built in the early 1700's. The wharf and the surrounding area were active with seafaring commerce in the Colonial era and upward of the nineteen-fifties. Commercial fishing and the sea freight industry became victims of the times and the area turned into a fish-stinky historic leftover.

Once most of the fishermen had drunk themselves to death, someone had the inspiration to create a shopping/dining/excursion boat area that covered about two blocks. The wharf was now upscale as well as historic. Clock Tower Condo Township was built by DiSpirito Construction, owned by Cassie's father. The first unit sold was to my very self.

Both condo and convertible were mine due to a generous settlement from the Eastern Fastrack Company, owing to the fact that a weighty piece of commuter rail had dropped from an overhead bridge and managed, among all of the heads in Massachusetts, to strike mine.

That morning I was walking along Federal Street toward my office and next I was awakening at Mass General Hospital.

Due to the head trauma I suffered, I'll never be completely right, but it's often been pointed out that I wasn't quite right anyway.

During my ten-day coma I had fever dreams that I rather enjoyed. I discussed relativity with Einstein (he wanted my views) and sang a couple of numbers with Janis Joplin. (I also played rhythm guitar quite passably on *Summer Time*.) I heard a steady beeping sound, which was somehow reassuring. In all, it wasn't unpleasant.

When I awoke, there were two pairs of eyes staring down at me – one dark brown pair belonging to an Asian doctor and the other very blue pair belonging to Cassandra DiSpirito. The staff had repeatedly asked her to leave and she had repeatedly stayed, shouting questions at me. When I regained consciousness, she was in my face saying, "Kitto, I know you can hear me!" I had heard this declaration many times before but had neither the inclination nor the ability to respond.

I tried to speak, but my mouth was dry and I had to run my tongue around the inside of my mouth and clear my throat a couple of times. Finally I managed to croak, "Shut the hell up," in a gurgling, gravelly voice. Cass jumped back and ran out of the room crying. Tubes were removed. The doctor leaned down and blasted a light into my left eye, which I didn't wholly appreciate. "How do you feel?" he asked solemnly.

I licked my lips again and swallowed a few times. "Uhm…sort of like half of my head was shot off. How do you feel?"

He aimed the light at my other eye, which annoyed me only slightly less than the first time, said nothing and left the room.

Cass returned with my mother and two of my brothers who had been lunching in the cafeteria. They were all talking at once and I held up my hand to quiet them. "If you were dividing up my possessions, I'll have to disappoint you."

My brothers don't cry, but they were looking at me with expressions I had never seen before. It was unnerving. My mother dabbed at her eyes and Cass was still blubbering.

"So, what exactly has happened here?" I asked uneasily, feeling the stubble on the top of my head that was growing out of some nasty incisions.

** **

My mother, Rose O'Hartigan, was the fifth of five girls. The first four were blue-eyed redheads but my mother appeared with raven locks and dark brown eyes. Their only brother, Patrick James (P. J.), could expound ad nauseam about her coloring being due to the sinking of the Spanish Armada off of the coast of Ireland a million years ago.

I have three older brothers -- Raphael, Michael and Uriel, named after archangels. This was my mother's doing. She especially enjoyed enlightening people about the archangel Uriel because no one in the world had ever heard of him. They saved Gabriel for last because my father and uncles concurred that it sounded, and here I quote, like a Heeb name. My father was delighted when I turned up female and the name became Gabriella, which had a fine guinea-wop ring. My mother, however, thought she had been dealt a bad hand when she was going for four of a kind.

My oldest brother, Raphael, has snapping brown eyes and curly black hair. He's quite good-looking and knows it. My father used to tell him that if he didn't behave, he'd hide all of the mirrors. Rafe thought us a family of dunces. It wasn't personal. He thought the same of nearly everyone. He nicknamed our mother "The Black Rose" in honor of some Irish anti-English war anthem involving treachery on the part of all involved.

Michael is a blue-eyed, light-haired version of Rafe, and his loyal lieutenant. They both delighted in misinforming Uriel (a/k/a "Doc") and me about nearly everything. I didn't know the correct rules to the simplest of games until my teen years, because the bros changed them every time I started to win. They told us both we were adopted and we believed it. We may have been secretly hoping that our real parents were coming to rescue us.

Uriel has dark curly locks like Rafe's, blue eyes like Michael's and is beyond adorable. When he was four years old, Santa brought him a toy doctor's kit. He kept it with him at all times in case of emergency, and failing that, he solemnly listened to hearts with the toy stethoscope and made people stick out their tongues so he could shove a Popsicle stick halfway down their throats and tell them to say "Ahhh," which was impossible to do. Since the older archangels had taken to calling him *Urinal,* it was for the greater good that the nickname "Doc" was the one that stuck.

My father, Del Labastiani, is a musician and singer and something of a local celebrity. He looked and sang a lot like Dean Martin, and was perfectly at home in a tux. He could pick up any musical instrument and play it. He taught me piano and guitar and he loved that I, unlike the boys, could harmonize with him. He tried to make us sing *Happy Birthday* in four-part harmony at every party, but my brothers would have none of it. I knew Doc could sing but he wasn't about to do so in front of his brothers.

My father called me "Kitten" because I used to look something like the little girl on *Father Knows Best.* We loved how Jim Anderson would come home from work and to chill out, he'd exchange his suit jacket for another suit coat with *patches.* In our neighborhood, a father would come home, take off a tee shirt and blow his nose on it.

Dad and I especially loved the episode where precious little Kitten deliberately lost a spelling bee so an unpopular kid could win. Dad and I both knew that I wouldn't have thrown a spelling bee for a kid with ten minutes to live. (I had once told my parents that I won all the spelling bees at school and my mother told me to stop bragging.) Eventually, Kitten was shortened to *Kit* and Gabriella Rose was relegated to the nuns or my mother when she was particularly displeased.

The youngest of the Black Rose's siblings and the only boy, was the darling of his parents and all of his sisters. Our generation called him Uncle Slug. He came by his nickname in the same tradition that a grandparent gets stuck with any demented-sounding name that a first-born toddler happens to burp up. I've heard grandparents lovingly called *Flumpy, Rancid* and *Crappy*.

When Raphael was a baby, my uncle had called him *Slugger* and once the little darling started talking, he called our uncle by that name (not that this made any sense.) My parents chose to immortalize the adorableness of this inaccuracy by continuing it.

While we were growing up, Uncle Slug lived on the first floor of our house with my grandmother and we lived on the second and third floors. Officially, he lived downstairs, but he could almost always be found at our kitchen table with a shot of VO, smoking Pall Malls, and pontificating. He was a town cop, so he knew everyone's sordid business and didn't mind sharing it. My mother and aunts were enchanted by his insider info. It assisted them greatly with knowing to whom they should (or should not) feel superior.

Uncle Slug had two verbal fallbacks: *Damn Skippy* when he was in agreement and *My Arse* when he wasn't. Grammy O. was even more consistent. She said *Deliver Me* when outraged, amused and everything in between.

The Black Rose lived her life on the brink of hysterical rage and moved as if she had been shot out of a cannon. The anger that strangles Irish people is probably due to having the boot of the English army on one side of their throats and the pointed papal slipper on the other forever. American Irish will weep hearing a song about a country that they've never seen, but recoil from the touch of a loved one.

Many Irish people will share your misery quite sincerely, but win the lottery and they'll be unable to conceal their contempt. Wishing people well isn't their long suit. In defense of the Irish, they were given a raw deal by the self-exalting English. As Grammy O. routinely informed us, centuries ago the evil English government sent Protestants to Northern Ireland to create and perpetuate tensions between them and the Irish Catholics. They were highly successful (although creating tensions with the Irish is not a difficult assignment), and those tensions continue to this day.

On God's behalf, Gram would snort, *"Protestants.* As if the Lord wants a new religion started very time the two of those *golram fools* disagree about a bake sale." It was her favorite speech. Another favorite of hers was singing the line, "And if I had a face like you I'd join the English army."

In my mother's insane view, you should be either ricocheting from one meaningful task to another or be sound asleep. (And here let us note that only the sleep you get before midnight does you any good.) You had to leave the house to relax since it wasn't an option inside of the house.

The archangels delighted in torturing me and imposing their overbearing maleness at every opportunity. For instance, I would enter my bedroom to find one of my dolls hanging by the neck from the Venetian blind cord, with her little nylon panties pulled down. My mother was appalled by the panties thing. I suspected that the hanging part should have troubled me more, were I the parent.

Another of their favorite cruelties was to shake me awake in the morning saying, *"Wake up...it's Christmas!"*...and it would be the middle of June. To be fair, Doc wasn't as evil as the older two, having been their favorite target before my arrival.

I attribute the mean streak that we siblings share to the Black Rose's example. Her idea of a compliment would be something like *Sheila isn't as homely as the rest of the Murphys*, and you would never convince her that this was *not* a compliment.

My mother's family had created a caste system in their minds whereby they would decide whether to look down on you for having less than they, or resent you for having more. Neither led to the establishment of warm friendships, and as a result, they never strayed far from each other socially.

Grammy O. and Uncle Slug were experts in assessing nearly every nationality on earth. In their worldview, the arrogance of the English and Jews was well-documented; Greeks were Jews with their brains kicked out and were suspicious of everyone, based on their own unseemly behavior; the French were rude, outspoken and ungrateful to us for bailing them out in two world wars; Armenians were thieves and all Italians were thugs who behaved absurdly when someone died. They cried, screamed and wailed. *Such carryings-on.* The thing to do when someone died was to make a custard. If a black family had moved in next door to our house, my uncle would have burned it down if my grandmother didn't do it first.

We called my Italian grandmother Yonni (another gift accredited to the endearing baby Raphael). She was about four feet tall and always had a broom in her hand. If she wasn't sweeping in the house, she would be sweeping the sidewalks or even the street. She attached religious medals to our shirts on a large safety pin when we went out to play, which my Irish mother later removed in disgust. The Black Rose asserted that this what Italian mothers did instead of actually raising their kids.

I remember that during the fallout shelter nonsense of the fifties, Grammy O. put two large cans of tomato juice in the cellar, firm in her belief that they would see our family through a nuclear holocaust. Michael and Rafe laughed hysterically and wrote their names on both cans, declaring that they would sit sipping while watching the rest of the family waste away from radiation sickness. Although in those days everyone did believe that the Russians and other communists were lurking everywhere with an atom bomb in each hand, gleefully awaiting the opportunity to annihilate the human race.

I, for one, believed them to be in league with the American food supply trade, since I had seen a picture of the soon-to-be-executed Rosenberg spies, and they looked suspiciously like the MacCauleys, the couple who owned the grocery store on Caldwell Avenue. I also suspected the Nissen Bread delivery men, because they seemed all too friendly with those owners – always talking, laughing, exchanging money. I was on to them, and I would stay awake at night, fearing that there could be such delivery men in their sneaky brown communist uniforms skulking outside our very house.

**

The Cavanaughs bought the house next to ours when I was four. They had been married for fifteen years and had only one child, Molly, and to my delight, she was exactly my age.

At first, Molly would play near the chain link fence that separated our properties and I would play in the same spot on my side of the fence. Neither of us spoke for a number of days. Finally, I threw a doll's head over the fence. She picked it up and took it into the house. The next day she threw it back over the fence, shouting "Hey!" which in the parlance of four-year-olds means "I'll be your best friend."

We marched off to kindergarten together. Unlike today, the parents didn't even go with you, much less hover over you, sobbing, until you felt comfortable. The following year, we entered the first grade at Our Lady Immaculata together.

Our Lady Immaculata was a parochial school that went from Grade One through (to our dismay), Grade Twelve. As teenagers, we envied the public high school students with their highly-funded sports programs and other civil liberties like going to different classes with different students. We got to sit in the same room all day while the tiresome nuns rotated from class to class. They were probably afraid that the girls would get pregnant should they walk past boys while changing classes.

Molly always had envied my having all those brothers. I did my best to convince her that it wasn't the blessing she thought it to be. Who did she think had caused the detaching of the doll's head? And that was minor in their annals of transgressions. But she loved the commotion in my house as much as I loved the tranquility in hers.

At dinnertime on my first day of elementary school, I announced with some importance that I had Sister Finn Faith for a teacher. The Archangels Raphael and Michael immediately informed me that she preferred to be called Sister Fishface and to make sure I did so. I had to admit that Fishface worked pretty well in her case, but my father told them both, *Zitto e mangia.*

**

Sister Abanathea was the principal of Our Lady Immaculata and the most feared of all the menacing nuns. The stupid cow had actually told our first-grade class, in the way of welcome, that we were expected to behave and to understand that our parents' love for us was greater than that of Catholic parents who sent their kids to public schools. I worried for my cousins who were quite happy not being ground through the angel factory but would eventually writhe in hell, along with their uncaring parents, for all eternity.

I must have appeared puzzled by this proclamation because Sister Abby's phony smile disappeared when she happened to look down at me. She rapped loudly on my desktop and I went cold with fear.

"What's your name?" she thundered.

"Kit," I managed to squeak.

She frowned. "You were baptized *Kit?*"

There were snickers from those of my classmates who thought it wise to pretend that Sister A. was witty.

"Gabriella," I corrected, once I remembered my name.

"Is that a first or last name?"

"My last name's Labastiani," I croaked.

This was a tactical error and I knew it the minute that it tumbled from my lips. My brothers were well-known, but not overly endeared to the administration of Our Lady. The nuns were insulting and cruel to little girls but they truly hated the boys, who weren't as easily bullied as the girls. My brothers were a particular nuisance because they were wiseasses who were also good students and athletes. It was not in the best interest of the school to toss them out. Raphael had figured that out pretty quickly and passed it on, by example, to the other archangels. There was a mutually resentful peace between the faculty and my siblings.

Sister Abby looked me up and down, shook her head and muttered, "Another Labastiani…" She got a few more laughs for that and moved down the row, seeking new victims.

A favorite among the Sister Abby legends was that of her catching Lorraine Collarusso and Kevin Muldoon holding hands in front of the school. The nun was so incensed by the sight of this puberty-fueled demonstration that she charged down the entrance walk, slapped Kevin across the face and shoved Lorraine – straight into the path of an oncoming garbage truck. Lorraine was thrown about twenty feet in the air before crashing down on the truck's hood. To add to this drama, the honey wagon, as garbage trucks were then dubbed, was driven by Lorraine's father.

The following day the good sister announced over the PA system that Lorraine's injuries were deserved, due to her wanton exhibition and for all of us to keep it in mind. Lorraine spent three weeks in the hospital and limped for the rest of her life, and it was just punishment for hand-holding, according to Sister Abby. I looked around the classroom and many heads were nodding in agreement that the punishment fit the crime.

**

We understood why the clock stoppers like Sister Fishface had taken the veil, but the few like Sister Mary Josephina had us stumped. Why such a woman chose to spend her life gazing at the hideousness of her fellow nuns and living an institutionalized life was incomprehensible.

We invented all manner of wild stories about what would have driven the woman to such a life choice: baldness, wooden leg, horrible scarring, all of which would be covered by the habit. Sister Mary Josephina was beautiful, even in her penguin suit and she was never nasty or insulting when she talked to a student. Unfortunately, nuns of her ilk were in the minority. She looked like Ingrid Bergman. Most of them looked more like Humphrey Bogart and acted like Attila the Hun. Sister Mary Josephina was proof that the meanness in the other nuns was a choice, and not a requirement.

CHAPTER

Port Locke, Massachusetts 1955

"We'll *play* with ya."

My brother Doc and I looked up from our game of sidewalk tic-tac-toe to see two young girls -- one about my age of seven and the other impossibly young.

"You the new kids?" Doc demanded skeptically. He inclined his head toward the top of the street where three new houses had been built, where there was once the woods that we had considered our rightful play property.

"Not that new," the older one said, looking down at her blue Cinderella watch nonchalantly as if she had much better places to be.

Doc snorted, picked up his chalk and banged up the front steps to 63 Madison. It was bad enough that he spent a lot of time with me, being frequently deserted by the older archangels, but he would not be found playing with three girls, one of whom was practically a baby.

The older girl watched him go, grabbed the younger one's hand and said, "Come on, let's get the hell out of here."

They walked. I quickly glanced up at the living room window to see if my mother was around. She had better hearing than most dogs and if she had heard this new girl swear, I'd get in trouble although I was neither talking nor swearing. Based on this and the fact that their new home had despoiled our erstwhile Sherwood Forest, I decided not to like this new girl whose stupid name was Cassandra.

After the bad start with my family's welcoming committee, Cassandra steered clear of me, but built up a following of her own, which I deeply resented. By the time we started the third grade, I realized that if we joined forces, we could rule the whole school.

**

Without signaling, the driver pulled into a truck-stop parking lot on Route 109. A flashing Budweiser sign had beckoned to him from yards away and he had braked suddenly. Tires screeched behind him and horns blared. He reached out of the window and held his middle finger up in front of the huge side mirror. His truck was bigger than all the cars on the road and that made him feel good.

He'd have a few well-earned pops, stay a while and if liked the vibe, the last delivery be damned. This sentiment crystallized as the first mouthful of golden brew slid down his unacceptably dry throat.

Four hours later, he staggered back to the truck and climbed up and into the cab. Driving home, his thoughts turned to his only child. The kid had better not give him any shit. He was a lot bigger than the kid, too. He chuckled as he lit up a Marlboro.

The boy heard the wheels crunching the graveled driveway and ran to the window of his second-story bedroom. He froze when he saw the cab of his father's truck towing a trailer behind. It meant that his father was drunk. He wasn't supposed to have the trailer attached to the cab at the end of the day. Once again, he had stopped somewhere, started to drink and elected not to make his delivery.

Next he would stagger in and bellow for the boy, who would do everything in his power not to upset him. Somehow he always managed to make him mad. Mad enough to punish him. No one was more creative than his father doling out punishment. Sometimes it seemed that the man enjoyed it. But the boy knew it was his fault. And even though he weighed every word, watched his tone and became next to invisible, he knew he deserved to be punished because he always made his father mad.

**

I had made a point of ignoring Cassandra for months and therefore had to think of a clever way to let her know that I had decided to grant her the privilege of being my friend.

Her house was at the top of our street, and like it or not, she had to walk by our house at 63 Madison twice a day during the school year.

Tossing a doll's head wouldn't be useful this time, so it was going to be necessary to "accidentally" run into her.

Having worked out my plan, I rushed home from school and didn't bother to change out of my hideous uniform, which I loathed. I jumped on my bike at the garage end of our long driveway and began to pedal madly, reaching the sidewalk at what I hoped was the right moment, and I careened around the hedges and nearly ran smack into Cass. I screeched to a stop and said "Oh, sorry -- are you all right? I didn't see you."

"It's okay," she replied, stepping around me and the bike, clearly wanting no conversation, and kept walking.

"Gotta bike?" I shouted after her. As if I didn't know she had a beautiful red three-speed English bike with hand brakes and a very cool electric horn.

She turned around and her eyes narrowed. "Why?"

"I have to go to the square. You wanna come?"

She answered quickly, as if we chatted like this every day and hadn't been avoiding each other like mortal enemies.

"Yuh, I guess so. I have to go to the paper store anyway."

**

"You're acting like a child," I told Molly.

"I'm eight years old, Kit. I *am* a child."

She was in a snit, as Grammy O. would say. I had created her discomfort by spending the day before with Cass DiSpirito.

"I just don't like her."

"Well, I do. We went to her grandfather's restaurant."

"Big deal. You've been to my father's restaurant."

"But we couldn't leave the kitchen and he made us peel potatoes. At Poppi's, we drank Cokes and played cards in one of the booths. It was fun."

Molly looked like she was sniffing something foul. "Well I still don't like her."

**

CHAPTER

Port Locke, Massachusetts

My uncle Slug's '58 Mercury hardtop was always waxed and buffed to a perfect shine by my brothers. He would never have allowed a car wash to have its way with the Mercury's paint. The archangels' efforts were rewarded with a ride down the causeway to the beach and an ice cream at Roland's on the way back. I was not allowed to participate because I was too young. Since there are exactly seventeen months between me and Doc, I suspected gender bias but I knew that I'd get nowhere on that issue.

The car was a deep burgundy with a spotless white top and was my uncle's favorite thing in the world. Accustomed to the pedestrian Chevy station wagon that Dad required for his band equipment, the Mercury looked like a spaceship to us. It had power windows and even the back window went down at the touch of a button. It was almost a *convertible* spaceship.

He drove it from 1958 to 1975 and heaven help the bird who was discourteous enough to deposit upon it. My uncle would throw stones skyward, and viciously attack the waste with cloth, paper and Glass Wax, spitting the oath, *"There are two things I hate and they're both pigeons."*

He and the Black Rose were witty. My aunts and uncles were, too, when you could catch them sober.

**

My friends and I didn't know the origin of the phrase "Goody Two Shoes" but Cass and I liked the sound of it and applied it to those of our classmates who were in our judgment, overzealous Catholics; in other words, all of them, including Molly.

"Hail Mary, full of grace, kick the ball and take your base," Cass unadvisedly hollered at one of the Cartelli twins who was cowering at home plate, waiting for the kickball to be pitched. The Cartellis weren't really twins. The older one was just stupider than the younger and they had ended up in the same grade.

All of the Two Shoes gasped in horror at Cass's blasphemy and I shared their pain when I spied the outraged face of Sister Abanathea in the window just above Cass's head. The nun's face looked uglier than normal and had turned an unhealthy-looking shade of red just before it disappeared from view. She thundered onto the playground through the basement door, grabbed Cass by the collar and dragged her back into the school. Sister F. immediately appeared, ringing her ridiculous bell like a woman possessed, signaling an early end to recess.

I flew up the stairs to our classroom where Sister A. was screaming at Cass to stand up in front of the class. Once everyone had rushed into their seats to better view the drama, the good sister announced, "Miss DiSpirito thinks she's a poet and she will now recite the Hail Mary ten times – if she remembers the correct words."

Cass had, along with her northern Italian blonde hair, the proverbial "peaches and cream" complexion, but at this moment, her face was purple with humiliation. Before carefully evaluating the consequences, I suddenly flung myself out of my chair and onto the floor with such vigor that I banged my head on the corner of Maureen Costello's desk, distracting Sister A. from the disciplinary proceedings, and she turned and stomped toward me, wild-eyed.

Fortunately, I had once witnessed an old man having a seizure on the Wonderland subway station platform. I made my body appear to convulse all over and thrust my tongue in and out of my mouth, causing alarming gagging noises and when the good sister's ugly black shoes were within reach, I proceeded to enthusiastically bite her in the ankle.

Once again demonstrating her great love of children, she kicked me in the face with her other foot and luckily my mouth began to bleed. Thus committed, I had to be willing to take this all the way to the Academy Awards ceremony. I freed her ankle and worked up as much saliva as I could, and mixed with the blood, it was quite effective when I sprayed the foamy mess out of my mouth.

The nuns were beginning to look concerned. I augmented my performance with a full body flip, landing on my face. By now there was complete pandemonium as all of my classmates were out of their seats and gawking, hoping to see someone actually croak in their little faces. I decided it would be a good time to lose consciousness, which I was quite good at, due to years of practice feigning sleep, going back to when my parents would drive us home at night from visiting and I would be "asleep" so that my father would carry me up the stairs.

I closed my eyes and waited for the Blessed Mother to appear and slap me around for committing a sin they probably didn't even have a name for, but she didn't show. And -- I had accomplished my goal of making everyone forget about Cass.

The price I paid was being hauled off to a bewildered doctor every year to check the epileptic condition that I didn't have. My mother ranted to my father that no one in *her* family had seizures. (The assigning of blame was another of the O'Hartigan sisters' principal duties.) Biting Sister A's ankle was well worth the doctor visits, and Cass was forever grateful.

This did nothing to improve the reputations of Misses Labastiani and DiSpirito, especially among our Irish Religious Nazi classmates who already viewed our behavior as less than Catholic. To this day, there are those who avoid exciting me, lest I pitch another fit and bite a nun.

**

Michael came up with yet another nickname for our mother, which was Our Lady of Perpetual Disappointment. If it wasn't bad enough that the Black Rose had been cheated out of her fourth archangel, she was further martyred by having a daughter with perfectly straight hair.

In the fifties this just would not do, and those of us who lacked curls were chased around by mothers wielding a horrid product called a Toni home permanent. It stunk up the house and made a child's straight hair into frizz while burning her tender scalp. It was considered just punishment for being curl-deficient.

Many of my generation became hair stylists for the sole purpose of getting back at their mothers by giving them frizzy perms in their old age. I have a friend who admits to burning the old girl's pink scalp and thinning grey hair on a weekly basis as retribution for those class pictures where we all looked like Art Garfunkle.

My mother had just finished inflicting this process and tied the Toni-supplied blue plastic around my head, which was probably intended to keep the smell from killing the birds in the sky.

Part of the murky design in the bathroom floor linoleum at our Madison Street home looked exactly like a cuddly teddy bear from one angle and a hideous death mask at another. Sometimes I could only see the teddy and others times only the ghoul was revealed in the exact same spot. It fascinated me and I was contemplating this phenomenon from my porcelain perch. It was hard to see either image because my eyes were watering due to the stench that was percolating under my plastic turban. To my horror, I heard Cass's voice outside the window, attempting something like a conversation with Raphael – the archest angel of them all.

"Where's Kit?" she demanded, causing me to freeze on the toity, thinking *Cassie, don't swear, don't swear, don't swear...*

From his metal lawn chair/throne on the back porch, Rafe casually responded, "The circus was in town and they took her."

"Dipstick," Cass enunciated very clearly. My brother got her meaning, but couldn't report to the Black Rose that my nasty little friend was being un-Catholic.

It was all power and mind games with Rafe. He certainly didn't care what I or any of my friends called him since in his world we were so much toe jam, but if he had potentially damning information (like friends who cussed) to hang over my head, it would be used wisely, and not quickly.

**

Cass and I went to Chamberlain's News Store every day after school to get the Green Sheet for her grandmother, who never worried about the change from her dollar and neither did we. Daily we treated ourselves to a bunch of penny candy, Hershey's or Three Musketeers Bars.

I thought my grandmothers were insane until I met Nonnie. Her full name was Yolanda Casabucci DiSpirito. She had deep frown lines between her eyes that made her look perpetually pissed off. She could usually be found atop a stool at their kitchen counter, agonizing over the Wonderland Daily Double picks, comparing her choices with both the Green Sheet and the Boston Record American handicappers' page. While she disapproved of her sister's son, Boochie the Bookie's chosen occupation; she saw no reason not to be loyal and patronized his business on a daily basis.

Nonnie always had a Kent cigarette burning down in a big black ash tray that was shaped like a miniature tire. I never saw her actually smoke one. She arose only to stir the ever-present pot of gravy. On the rare occasions that she smiled, her face changed completely and she was beautiful.

One of the few times I saw her actually laugh was when Cass told her that an Italian on the Mike Douglas Show had said that the only pretty word in the English language was *cellar door*. Nonnie agreed and howled with laughter.

Cass's father had a younger sister named Angela who lived with them, along with Nonnie and Poppi. She was only six years our senior and we thought she was the epitome of fifties cool. She bought all the hit records, stacked them on her 45 rpm record changer and we would all sing along and swoon over the works of Elvis, Fabian, Sam Cooke and Frankie Avalon, among others. She gave Cass those record sleeves that had the artist's picture on them to tack up on her bedroom walls.

Angie taught us the dances of the day. Doing The Stroll, The Hand Jive and The Walk required no actual dancing ability. Anyone with limbs could do them, but we thought we looked impossibly cool executing these moves.

Angie and her friends wore their dungarees rolled up and their cardigans buttoned up the back. They put Vaseline on their eyelashes to make them grow and stole cigarettes from every available purse and pocket. She gave me my first smoke, and I'm still grateful.

Whenever the TV commercial for The Ozzie and Harriet Show that was shown every twenty seconds began, regardless of her whereabouts, Angie would come barreling into the living room at the first strum on the guitar. Ricky Nelson would then sing a line of his hit *Poor Little Fool* in which he claimed that he had been a fool. In response, she would cover her ears and moan, "You were not...you were not!" Immediately following, Angie would slump into a heap, emotionally drained. Despite Ricky's bad judgment in sweethearts, Angie was passionately in love with him, as were a few million other teenaged girls.

Cass's grandfather, Poppi, made red wine in the DiSpirito basement. He filled quart-sized Coca Cola bottles with it and covered the tops with tin foil. The wine was served at his restaurant and those who partook of it left staggering. To fuel this endeavor, Poppi had created a huge grapevine network behind the DiSpirito house. The arbor had a built-in wooden bench with a trellis over the top. When it filled in with huge grape leaves, it created a shady, concealed fortress that we loved.

In early summer, we ate the green grapes that were so sour they made your glands explode and as the season progressed, the grapes turned purple and sweetened. We thought it an excellent pastime to put the purple ones in our mouths and squish the inner globs out of the skins, then move them around on the tongue, imagining that they were alien eyeballs.

We spent a lot of time playing there in our childhoods and as adolescents, exchanging erroneous information about sex. For instance, we had been told that someone knew someone who knew a girl who had been born with a glass bottle inside of her that caused her to bleed for a few days every month. We believed this tragic story much longer than we should have.

**

It was the week before our First Holy Communion ceremony and I had swiped a pocket knife from the bedroom of the younger archangels. At age eleven, Raphael had insisted upon having a bedroom to himself in the attic, away from his younger, unsophisticated siblings.

With the aid of this tool, Cass and I pried open two penny-candy flying saucers, both sides of which passed nicely for a communion wafer. They also stuck to the roof of your mouth unpleasantly like the wafer. After removing and savoring the silver candy beads, we donned our veils and I knelt on the floor while Cass administered the Eucharist to me.

Then it was her turn, and while she was kneeling with her tongue sticking out, my mother entered the room unheard and suddenly made a noise like someone who had just been pierced by a harpoon. I turned to see her face go white in horror. She choked when she tried to speak and motioned toward the door. Cass, who was quite relieved by the invitation to leave, looked back in sympathetic sorrow as she disappeared out the door. She thought my mother had actually gone insane. There wasn't much in the way of discipline at the DiSpirito house. When they were getting bawled out, it was hard to tell, because everyone in the house yelled all the time, except Tina. Cass wasn't familiar with my mother's brand of icy Irish ire, where a broken eggshell provokes the exact same reaction as hearing that your entire family has been tortured and strangled. Molly's mother was also Irish and acted just like mine, and Cass didn't even try to figure them out.

It wasn't a pleasant evening although the archangels got quite a chuckle out of it. The Black Rose threatened to have me barred from receiving communion forever – a penalty with which I probably could have lived. She punctuated her outrage by stating that Cass and I together didn't equal half an idiot and I was to stay away from her. I nodded and held my tongue, but I knew that was not going to happen.

**

CHAPTER

Port Locke, Massachusetts

The boy knew that it would be a bad night, but had managed to drift off to sleep. When the creaking of his bedroom door opening awoke him, he sat up and saw his father staggering toward his bed, reeking of alcohol. The smell turned the boy's stomach.

He was sick of his father's smell, sick of his own fear and sick of his father's "punishments."

Catching the man off balance he screamed, "No!" -- leaped out of the bed and shoved him backward. He ran past the drunken man, who swiped at him belatedly and missed. He ran into the hall and down the stairs. When he dared to stop and look back, he saw his astonished father teetering at the top of the stairs.

"When I get you, you little bastard..." he slurred and took a step forward, misjudging the top stair.

He seemed to hang briefly in mid-air before crashing down the entire flight of stairs, banging his head on the floor, making a sickening crack.

The boy backed against the wall and waited for the fool to come around. Now he'd really be mad. But a few minutes went by and he didn't move. A bright red puddle began to form beside his head.

He watched in horror...then fascination. Finally he sat down on the couch opposite where his father lay and watched him bleed to death.

**

CHAPTER

Bamberg, Germany

The beautiful child ran happily ahead of Anke, tripped over a tree root and fell flat on his face. After that momentary silence during which a child assesses the damage to his or her person, a wail followed, indicating more indignation than pain. Anke hurried to pick him up and rocked him in her arms. He had his mother's coloring -- startlingly blue eyes, pink cheeks and hair the color of the sun. Anke gently wiped the forest debris from his tiny palms and kissed his forehead.

As she soothed him, she heard a cracking noise from somewhere in the woods behind them. She quickly put him on hit his feet, bent down and said, "Emil, the road is over there," gesturing toward the West. "I want you to go the road and run. Run as fast as you can to Aunt Magda's house. Can you do that?" He looked confused and frightened but nodded his head solemnly.

"Tell Aunt Magda that I'm going to church," she said. He looked puzzled, but she gave his back a gentle push and said, "Go!"

Emil began to walk, then run, glancing back doubtfully over his shoulder. Anke smiled and waved him on with a cheerfulness she didn't feel. There was another snapping sound from the woods, closer this time.

Her blue eyes looked heavenward for a long moment. Then she walked with resignation to a large rock, sat down and waited.

**

CHAPTER

Port Locke, Massachusetts

During our childhood, Doc and I knew that when Uncle Slug took us out on a Saturday afternoon, we would end up at the Gallivan American Legion Post #444. We loved *The Post,* as it was affectionately referred to as by Uncle Slug and his pals, all of whom were cops or crooks. Some were both. The Post offered pinball, bowling machines and soggy pizza for us and twenty-five-cent beer for him.

I commandeered the jukebox and played the same records over and over with nickels supplied by my increasingly happy uncle. The vets were having none of Elvis or what they called "jungle bunny" music, but I loved hearing songs like *Moments to Remember* by the Four Lads and *Love Letters in the Sand* by Pat Boone. I could even tolerate an occasional Perry Como (*Catch a Falling Star*) or Dean Martin (*That's Amore*) effort.

Later he would tell the Black Rose that we went bowling (which wasn't exactly a lie) or that we had gone for a ride after lunch (also somewhat true.) One day he took us to the dump and let us fire at tin cans, while he took aim at the occasional rat, to our revulsion. We were sworn to death-penalty silence about that or there would have been another Irish Black Rose uprising.

It was also a fine adventure when Cass and I accompanied Poppi to his restaurant in East Boston (or Eastabost, as Uncle Slug called it), on Saturdays. The walls of the Pastabello were adorned with picture puzzles that had been glued together and framed by a patron. One picture was a beautiful Sicilian village and the rest were of semi-clad females in various poses of implied cooperation. Years of smoke and grease had given them a gauzy look that sort of looked like it had been done on purpose.

The gimmick at Poppi's restaurant was that when he got a complaint about the food, which was rare, he would invite the complainant into the kitchen to correct whatever it was that he or she saw as a problem. He would announce to the cooks that there was an expert in the house to help them out. Said expert usually apologized and fled.

If a drink wasn't made strong enough for a patron's taste, Poppi would make him open his mouth and pour whiskey or the appropriate liquor down it until the patron changed his mind. People thought this was great. Nino DiSpirito was a small, cocky guy who was pretty sure that no one would assault him and his eatery became a popular tourist attraction.

He let us sit behind the bar and dispense endless Cokes from the machine and we felt highly privileged. We also got to eat our fill of our favorite meatballs and ravioli plate.

If a patron had the bad taste to ask Poppi for pizza, he made a spitting noise and told them to go the North End where they served the phony Italian food. Patrons loved that, too, even though it wasn't even true.

Poppi worked there six days a week and closed on Mondays. If he wasn't there, *they'd-a steal-a you blind.* When he and Nonnie married, he promised her she would never work. She readily agreed and worked her kitchen while he worked his.

**

Cass and her sisters looked almost exactly alike; like the same person wearing different colored wigs. Cass was blonde, Gina's hair was auburn and little Tina's hair was so black, it was blue.

Gina was an okay kid for a younger sister. She idolized Cass and frequently followed us around. Since we were usually up to something reportable, we elected to draw her into our confidence, hoping she'd keep her trap shut and she did. Being the middle child, she developed a great sense of humor to keep from being overlooked, and she was a hoot. She told the frizzy-haired Mr. Tarmello at the newsstand that he reminded her of Bozo the Clown. She thought it was a compliment. He didn't. She had also informed Nonnie that she was a lot less ugly with her teeth in.

With Tina, the combined genes had come close to perfection. She was tiny, unlike her sisters, and had huge dark eyes, but her other features were just like Gina's, who looked just like Cass. Her hair was shiny and never looked messy. Her voice was sweet and barely audible. Once, when Cass and I had taken her to MacCauley's Market, Mrs. Mac gave her a lollipop. When she said, "Thank you for the Tootsie Pop," the woman was amazed.

"She can talk like that?" Mrs. Mac marveled.

To which Cass replied, "I hope to hell she can talk. She's seven years old."

**

I still clearly remember that afternoon after school that Cass and Molly were at my house watching *American Bandstand*. The Highwaymen's recording of "Michael Row the Boat Ashore" was new and after the show, I took out the third-hand guitar I had insisted upon receiving for my ninth birthday. I tentatively struck a G chord and the three of us forcefully sang, *Michael, row the boat ashore, alleluia...*in *perfect* three-part harmony. We stopped and looked at each other in amazement.

My father ran in from the kitchen "Was that you?" he demanded.

Next Grammy O. banged up the stairs with her mouth open and no words coming out – for once. She stood and stared.

"Do it again!" my father enthused.

We did. Cass sang the lead and Molly and I did the harmony and it was just as good as the first time. (Cass never understood how Molly and I knew how to harmonize and we never understood how she didn't.)

After that day we made actual music. In later years, I performed now and then with one or both of them, but mostly alone – especially as we got older and Molly was more interested in *finding herself* and Cass couldn't be trusted to show up for gigs. It was more fun performing with them or with my brother Doc, but I had to love being in a club, drinking, singing and playing the guitar. What could be a better deal than getting paid for what you would have been doing anyway?

Later that same day, Cass and I were sitting on the bench in Poppi's grapevine reading comics, which we knew we were getting too old for, but weren't quite ready to hang up. Suddenly she announced that she wouldn't live to be old. I waited for the joke; then realized that she was serious.

"Why do you think that?" I asked.

With a straight face she answered, "It's just something that I know."

"Why would you know that? You don't know anything else," I pointed out.

That seemed to bring her around she laughed and said, "Let's go get some candy."

"Can't. I don't have any money."

"You don't need any," she assured me.

Cass's ease with stealing things horrified me. She had learned the art from Nonnie, whose philosophy was *if they didn't want you to have it; they wouldn't have left it there.*

Twice a year, Nonnie left her kitchen stool and Daily Doubles for the Shirley Avenue outlet shoe stores in Revere. The most popular store was so small that it held about six people at a time while everyone else stood waiting in a line outside of the store. This did nothing for Nonnie's disposition, which wasn't all that sunny to start with. Once she gained entrance, she would simply put on new shoes, place her old ones in the box and put the box back on the rack. She would then stomp out, wearing the new shoes while muttering, "Madone, they got-a nahting..." Cass had learned from a pro.

I rarely accompanied Cass into Nelly's Corner Store on her capers, although I had no problem sharing in the bounty. Mostly I was just chicken, but if I got caught stealing, I would have to listen to Uncle Slug hold forth until I would be forced to take his gun and shoot him. P. J. O'Hartigan was, after all, an officer of the law, as frightening as that was.

**

CHAPTER

Bamberg, Germany

Magda heard the child before she saw him. A voice as sweet as a songbird's called her name from the east side of the cottage.

She hooked the serving ladle onto the side of the stew pot that simmered in the shallow fireplace and walked outside. Emil ran to her, smiling. She bent down and hugged him.

"Where's your mother... hiding?" she laughed, shading her eyes and searching behind him.

Emil broke from her embrace and looked up at her. He frowned, and she asked again, more urgently.

"Emil, where is Anke?"

He opened his mouth, closed his blue eyes and burst into tears.

**

CHAPTER

Port Locke, Massachusetts

There were six girls in my Immaculata class named Mary Veronica. Mary, of course, for the Blessed Mother, and Veronica for the woman who reportedly wiped Christ's face with her veil at the crucifixion, upon which was left an imprint of his face. It was clear to the Irish that naming children could be another couple of holes punched in your ticket to heaven, if you did it properly.

I also knew more than one fair colleen among us whose mother claimed a maiden name of Kelly when they had in fact (and through no fault of their own) names that sounded Scottish or worse, English. Every Irish woman who found herself in that unseemly position magically became a Kelly.

**

Auburn hair like Cass's sister Gina's is beautiful. There is, however, another shade of copper-like red that gives its bearer a goldfish look. These people usually have very light eyelashes, which contributes to the fish thing. There lived, on Upper Church Street, a family of such creatures named Boynton. Not only were they hideous, they were hateful little troublemakers.

As Cass and I, doing our age-thirteen version of cool, strolled past the Monroe School playground to the beat of Del Shannon's "Runaway" that was blasting from both of our transistor radios, Gina came screaming out of the park beside the school.

"Cassie! The Boyntons are ganging up on Tina."

Cass and I exchanged incredulous looks. This was akin to slapping a bunny rabbit. Cass grabbed Gina's arm and demanded, "Where are they?"

They started to run toward the dugout of the baseball field. I followed, ready to kill.

We reached the dugout to find four of the tribe of Boyntons, two girls and two boys much older and larger than Tina, encircling her. They were laughing and pointing while she stood in the center of the group, her huge eyes bright with tears.

"Come on, it's a party – dress up!" One of the boys put Tina in a headlock while the other pulled the bottom of her skirt up.

Cass flew past me, grabbed the boy and threw him against the back wall of the dugout. He banged the back of his head and slid down the wall to the bench.

His sister, who was a few years our junior warned us weakly, "You better leave him alone…"

Cass turned around, her face white with rage. She grabbed the Boynton girl by the neck and threw her against the back of the dugout. She landed next to her brother and they both stared stupidly at Cass. The intensity of her anger had shut everyone up, even me. The other two Boyntons, in a touching display of family loyalty, fled.

I picked up Tina, who had stopped crying and was looking with interest at what was taking place between her older sister and her tormentors. Cass leaned toward the cowering Boyntons and warned, through clenched teeth, "Don't ever go near my sisters again."

The boy nodded his head in earnest agreement and his sister nodded once. I leaned toward them, still holding Tina.

"Tell Tina you're sorry, like good little goldfish."

They both mumbled something like apologies and we turned to go. When I looked back from the other side of the park, neither Boynton had moved from the dugout.

Later, back at her house, Cass was still vibrating with anger. She said she had never been that mad in her life.

"Well, Tina's so little..." I began.

"That's not it. When there's a gang picking on just one, it drives me insane."

Actually, it had.

**

Having a huge component of my personality relate to both Cass and Molly didn't guarantee that they would relate to each other, and they didn't. This often led to my being pulled painfully in two different directions. For instance, upon arriving at the beach, one of my dear pals would walk to the left and the other to the right. Often I just walked straight ahead, sat down and waited for them both to cut the crap and come back.

One memorable Saturday afternoon when we were in the tenth grade, Molly, Cass and I – as well as another friend named Dottie Moscella -- went to see the movie *Goldfinger*, largely because it was on the MORALLY OBJECTIONABLE IN PART FOR ALL section of the list posted at the back of the church. For what more of an endorsement could we ask? As always, Molly wanted to sit near enough to the front to break her neck while watching and Cass wanted to sit in the back row and do evil things. I compromised by commanding that we stop about halfway down the aisle and announcing loudly, "Right here's good."

Molly stopped and genuflected before she entered the empty row. Without thinking, I also genuflected, as did Dottie and then Cass. Once we sat down and realized what we had done,

Molly, Dottie and I proceeded to laugh through two movies, previews of coming attractions and a cartoon. Cass, however, was profoundly humiliated to think she had done such an un-cool thing in the presence of only-God-knew-who. And of course, she blamed Molly for leading us down that ridiculous path of righteousness.

Cass was still spitting nails at her uncle's pizza shop after the movie. "Goddam it, can you imagine what a bunch of prude-y little Catholics we must have looked like?" she demanded. "Jesus H. *Christ.*" She always ramped up the cursing when she wanted to annoy Molly.

I tried soothing her by saying, "Who cares, Cass? If anybody saw us, they'd probably just think we were kidding around." She made a face and continued to pout.

"Since when do you care so much about what you look like?" Molly laughed. "You, who mooned the boys' choir practice."

Cass glared. "Well, that was *my* idea," bitterly resenting what a joy it was for Molly to know that she was aggravated as hell.

Midmorning on the following Monday, Sister/Principal Abanathea solemnly entered our class room. Sister Fishface nearly fell over backward at the sight of her. When she had recovered and had sweetly sung out, "Good morning, Sister," she turned to us with at a look that would wither a Samurai warrior. We all jumped out of our seats and echoed "Good morning, Sister" in very holy tones. The principal nodded and then began to speak quietly, with great sorrow.

"I have been told," and here she paused for effect and looked to the heavens, "that over this weekend, there were students of this school seen at a movie theater making *mock* of the church."

There were gasps among the faithful. Every student in class looked puzzled, except for my friends and my fine self, who looked merely angelic. Sister F. turned back to the class in shock, gazing up and down the rows in the hope that the perpetrators, if present, had been turned to stone.

Sister A. stood quietly with her hands up her sleeves or wherever it is that they hid hands, and waited. If she thought the guilty would break from the silence, she didn't know the guilty. I was a little nervous about Dottie, because I knew that her uncle on her mother's side was a priest, suggesting that she might weaken and beg forgiveness, but she didn't. Molly's mouth was petrified shut, Cass didn't give a flying fig and I was greatly entertained by anything that upset nuns. I just had to keep from letting it show. We began to look around the room like the other students, avoiding eye contact with each other, which would have blown the whole thing. Finally the good Sister rose theatrically and took her somber leave.

If there was one thing that Catholicism had taught us, it was that all confession will get you is penance.

**

The following weekend, Cass appropriated a bottle of Poppi's wine and I a pack of my mother's Tareytons (from which you'd rather fight than switch) and we sat beneath the grape leaves chain-smoking and gulping the hallucinogenic wine.

There was a statue of Saint Francis of Assisi at the back of the grapevine. At some point, the bird that sat on his right hand had either changed religions or flown away, leaving what appeared to be the middle finger of the good saint extended. We loved it and lived in fear that Poppi would notice and correct the situation. We had always been amused by it, but on this particular night it seemed impossibly funny.

To this merriment, Cass added, "You know how my relatives in East Boston stick a bathtub upside down in the ground and put a saint in it to protect the house?"

"Uh-huh. My relatives do it too. It drives my mother insane. I mean *more* insane."

"Well, how about this? My Uncle Marco's house got robbed and instead of buying an alarm system, he strung some Christmas lights around Saint Anthony's bathtub."

"Oh, that'll scare the crooks away. You know what my brothers call the one where the bathtub is painted blue and they stick in a statue of the Blessed Mother?"

"No, what?"

"Mary on the half shell."

Cass proceeded to laugh while sipping, causing red wine to blast out of both of her nostrils, and that finished me. I collapsed on the bench, alternately laughing and begging her to do it again.

The late-night bout of vomiting on our jammies did nothing to dissuade us from thinking that this had been an excellent evening overall.

**

CHAPTER

Bamberg, Germany

She wouldn't give them fear. The Sight had shown her where this would lead and that couldn't be changed; but if she screamed, it would be only from pain, not fear.

"Have you ever seen this woman?" Prince Bishop Schelt demanded of Braithe, the simpleton farmer who stood before him in the huge chapel anteroom.

The filthy man nodded enthusiastically. "Near the caves in the Hawkswood."

"Liar," Anke said quietly.

The guard who was standing behind her raised his sword and struck her back with the handle. Her knees buckled, but she stayed on her feet. Looking mildly annoyed, the bishop continued, "What was she doing?"

"Dancing around a fire, singing like," Braithe said, showing what was left of his green teeth. "No clothes," he added, giggling.

The bishop nodded his approval at the farmer and then sighed knowingly. Anke laughed and shook her head in disbelief.

Ignoring her, the bishop announced, "She is to be examined for the mark of the witch."

"And if you don't find one, you'll make one," she countered softly.

"This impudence will not serve you, wench."

Schelt motioned to one of the two witnessing priests, to hand him an iron hand tool. He reached down and pulled Anke's shift up over her head roughly. She crossed her arms over her chest, attempting to cover herself, but the guard grabbed both of her arms and held them behind her back.

The bishop began to run the tool slowly down Anke's neck, then over her shoulders. Using the tool to lift each of her breasts, he carefully examined the flesh beneath. He then ran the tool down the front of her torso and suddenly inserted it into her. She gasped from the pain and the bishop sneered and turned to the priest on his left.

"The witch enjoys this. She doesn't know that her trickery is wasted on a man of God."

The priest agreed most vigorously, eyeing Anke with disgust. The bishop then removed the tool from her body as savagely as it had been inserted, and she staggered slightly. The bishop took hold of her arm to steady her and she turned to him calmly and spit in his face.

They were all too stunned to move. Wiping the spittle from his face, the bishop shouted, "Blasphemer!" and slapped the side of her head with all of his strength. She fell to her knees, but immediately raised her head.

"Who other than Satan could make a woman behave this way?" Schelt demanded. Turning to Braithe, he said "As her accuser, you choose. Fire or stone?"

"Fire" the farmer replied dreamily. "She likes fire," and again his idiot laughter filled the huge room.

The prince bishop's work was done.

**

CHAPTER

Port Locke, Massachusetts

"Molly, I don't think you fully grasp the concept of truancy," I told my friend while Cass convulsed with laughter on her bed.

"You actually asked for permission to skip school?" Cass asked between guffaws.

Cass and I had been planning a Christmas shopping spree for a school day when we could avoid the pesky weekend crowds. Molly agreed to join us, but only with parental permission, which she had somehow managed to secure. Cass thought this was the most ridiculous thing she had ever heard and that it was proof positive that Molly was the biggest Two Shoes that ever lived. Molly got touchy about the hilarity and announced that she was not skipping with us and went to school.

"Well," I chuckled to Cass, "she finally did something defiant. She told her parents she was skipping school and went anyway."

Cass put on a mock fearful face and said, "Think they'll ground her for this?"

"Maybe they'll just make her do a makeup skip day." We laughed all the way to the shopping center.

**

"Shit, there's Chickie Delvecchio," Cass whispered as she shoved me behind a column in the accessories department of Sears Roebuck.

"So?"

"So I don't want her to see me like this."

"Like what?" She looked like she had just stepped off of the cover of Vogue. Cass was sporting Frye leather boots, black cord knickers, a black cashmere sweater and a short suede jacket that was an unlikely shade of lavender. This ensemble was apparently unsuitable for unexpected viewing by Diana "Chickie" Delveccio who was the only known threat to Cass's status as World's Best Dressed.

"What's she wearing?" Cass hissed at me.

"How should I know? I can't see through this post."

"Don't move."

"All day?"

Suddenly, from our left we heard, "Kiiiiiiiiit...Caaaaaaasss... hey, what are you doing?"

"Hiding from you, bitch," Cass mumbled just before she raised her hand to wave and shout, "Chickie...Hi...Do you get all of your clothes at Sears?"

**

Cass and her boyfriend, Gordon Coelridge Wells the Third, (a/k/a the Turd) had been an item, off and on, since the age of fifteen. He was blonde, handsome, funny, and pretty much the male version of her. Individually they were dangerous, and together they were highly combustible.

Gordo was the offspring of two people (Gordon Coelridge Wells, Junior and Mary Elizabeth Colby), who thought anyone who wasn't a WASP (White-Anglo-Saxon-Protestant) should be outside plowing WASP fields or inside (wipe your feet, please) polishing WASP silver.

They considered their son's dalliance with the daughter of an Italian contractor with possible mob times (didn't they all?) an effrontery to his lineage. They were further scandalized by his choice to work construction for Cassie's father rather than participate in his father's business, which appeared to be the counting and fondling of money.

The volatile Cass and Gordo pairing broke up frequently; sometimes with good reason and other times just for the hell of it. Neither was dedicated to the concept of personal fidelity, but demanded it unequivocally from the other.

When we were in high school, several different people had seen Gordo squiring a certain young lady around the Italo-American Carnival. Said young lady was not Cass. When confronted, he delivered the memorable line:

"Who are you going to believe...me or the people who saw us there?"

This was problematic for Cass, who didn't care to break up because it was the week before her birthday. It was also problematic for me because I would have to listen to the breakup sorrow and grief when I knew damn well they'd be back together in a week.

"Maybe he meant to say the people who *said* they saw them?" she ventured.

"Yuh...probably...maybe," I said while thinking, *of course four people who weren't even together had the exact same hallucination.*

**

Molly was a pretty good keyboard player. This talent had afforded her the highly un-cool privilege of playing the organ at the nine o'clock Sunday Mass. She strictly forbade the presence of Cassandra and myself at these gigs, which made us all the more anxious to be there to support her. We respected her wishes for two Sundays in a row, but on the third, we quietly climbed the thousand stairs to the choir loft and sat directly behind the organ bench. We knew she wouldn't turn around in church because it was a sin.

We sat there quietly until the end of the mass. Molly began playing the last hymn, *Holy God, We Praise Thy Name*, and Cass got up, leaned over and began playing the right hand melody part of *Heart and Soul* on the upper keys. Once Molly realized what was happening, she slapped at Cass's hand, but *Heart and Soul* prevailed for quite a few measures, throwing Molly's timing off and while she was still on *all on earth thy scepter claim*, the bewildered congregation was already on *Lord of all we bow before thee*. This confusion caused them to sound like they were singing, *We bow-wow before thee.*

This accomplished, Cass quickly joined me at the top of the stairs and we made good our escape. Once outside, we hid in Cass's father's Cadillac across the street from the church. When Molly emerged a few minutes later, Father Inn (actually his name was Father Winn, but we preferred the reference to a dirty joke that we'd heard in the first grade) caught up with her and stopped her halfway down the stone steps. He was gesturing wildly in the direction of either the choir loft or God in heaven and Molly was visibly disintegrating.

"That man has *zero* sense of humor," Cass observed. She was lying down on the huge front seat with just enough of her head showing to be able to see Molly. I had assumed the same position in the back seat.

"He also has no ear for music. You and Molly played very well together."

"Damn skippy," she answered, borrowing Uncle Slug's phrase.

Molly had turned away from the priest and started to walk toward the Caddy. We both ducked down further, suggesting perhaps, that the car had come to the church on its own. When Moll knocked on the passenger window, we sprang from our respective lookouts and Cassie lowered the power window and purred, *"Hiiiiii Moll..."*

Molly yanked the gigantic car door open and plunked down on the passenger seat, looking pale and distressed.

"Drive!" she ordered and Cass, for once, was obedient. She started the engine, roared out of the parking spot and drove about five blocks before pulling over in front of her uncle's nice safe pizza shop and out of the sight and reach of church personnel.

Suddenly Molly's shoulders started shaking and I leaned over from the back seat, touched her shoulder and said, "Aw, Moll, don't cry."

Cass and I exchanged sheepish looks. This was a little more than we had been going for. It took several minutes for us to realize that Molly wasn't crying or convulsing.

"We *bow wow* before thee," Moll hiccupped, laughing loudly.

Much relieved, Cass and I joined in the jollity and soon we were all at the mercy of that helpless mirth than can that can only be attained by teenaged girls. It causes actual pain and could probably kill you.

The next day Molly's musical privileges at Immaculata were revoked, but Cass and I had a new respect for her and *Holy God*, was it worth it.

**

CHAPTER

Port Locke, Massachusetts 1968

"Isn't it a fine thing to send your kids to a Catholic college so they can come home and inform you that there's no God," the Black Rose fumed at Michael and Raphael.

This was in response to Rafe's dinner table declaration that the only thing religion was good for was keeping the poor from the throats of the rich. Oh, and Karl Marx was right about socialism being the perfect form of government. Rafe knew that this kind of talk drove Uncle Slug and my father insane. They had both served in World War II and were somewhat emotional on the subject of freedom.

"Your day will come, Boyo," Uncle Slug told Rafe. Dad smiled and nodded his head. However, a few years later, when Rafe and Michael were drafted and more than likely going to Vietnam, both father and uncle were not particularly enthused.

The other archangels never disagreed with Rafe, and any time that I had challenged him, he had quite effectively shredded my logic. I picked my battles carefully.

Even so, inspired by one of J. D. Salinger's books, I had read about four sentences on the subject of Zen Buddhism and deemed it to be my path and destiny. One evening at dinner, believing that my new, expansive spirituality required me to instruct the less enlightened, I offered "Maybe God just isn't a Catholic."

My mother shot me a look that should have prompted the warning not to freeze that way, but I thought better of that.

"Buddha..." I began and everyone at the table broke up.

"BUDDHA!" Rafe snorted.

More laughter.

I retreated. My family wasn't ready for enlightenment.

**

Following a mixer at State, our friend Patty Donnelly had the bad luck to get pregnant during an LSD-induced bout of lust with a co-ed that she couldn't name.

Her mother, who was the most sadistically Catholic of all of our mothers, was sorely tempted to buy Patty's story of seeing a vision of the Blessed Mother (also acid-induced) who had announced to her during this holy procedure that she too would conceive without sin.

Mrs. Donnelly had nearly fainted when Pat said she'd "just have an abortion." Abortion wasn't legal, but everyone knew a medical type who could get the job done.

"I just need two hundred dollars," Pat stated reasonably.

"Abortion!" Mrs. Donnelly fumed. "We're Catholics and we don't believe in abortion."

She also didn't believe in having an unwed pregnant daughter and couldn't be held responsible for any decisions made if all she had done was leave some money lying around. Say, about two hundred dollars.

**

What the hell for?" Cass demanded.

Molly had just announced that she'd like us to drive to Ipswich on this fine sunny day and let her stop at a phone booth to look up John Updike's name in the phone book. Assuming my unwanted role of mediator, I said, "Moll, it probably won't be in there and even if it is, are you gonna *call him?"*

"No. I just want to see his name."

"Once again," Cass said, "what the hell for?"

Molly sighed heavily and rolled her eyes. "Cass, he's a very famous writer, and he lives in Ipswich."

"And looking at his name in the phone book will do something for you?"

"Forget it. You don't understand," Molly sniffed.

Since I was the peacemaker, and the driver, I instructed kindly, "Shut up, both of you. We're just burning up gas anyway. Ipswich is as good a place as any."

With my two friends sneering at each other, I drove to Ipswich and stopped at a phone booth in the center of town. Molly and I opened the directory that was hanging by a theft-proof chain therein to find Underwoods and Uphams, but no Updike. She placed a dime in the slot and asked the operator for John Updike's number. *I'm sorry, that number is unlisted...*

"Hey Moll, try Mark Twain!" Cass yelled through the car window when she saw that there was no progress. Then she added, "Maybe the phone books are chained because John Updike keeps stealing all the ones that have his number in them."

"I could just smack her sometimes," Molly observed.

"And I could smack you both, *all* the time," I responded.

**

CHAPTER

Bamberg, Germany

At midnight, the captain of the guard spat an apple core out of his mouth and beckoned to his subordinate.

"You can go," he said gruffly.

The younger man was bewildered.

"Now?"

"Yes, I have some work to do." He laughed nastily and winked.

The soldier was close enough to smell the foul breath of the speaker and nearly gagged. The captain motioned with his head toward the prisoner's cell and shoved the young soldier out of his way. He removed the torch from beside the cell door and entered. Anke regarded him calmly.

He turned and shoved his sword through the door handles on the cell door to prevent interruption. Smiling, he slowly removed his armor plate and then his tunic. He approached Anke, grabbed her by the hair and yanked her up from her dirty bed of hay and rags.

She made no cry of protest and there were no tears. Her torture went on until dawn.

**

CHAPTER

Boston, Massachusetts

"We're three little lambs who have lost our way, baa baa baa," Molly, Cass and I bellowed in our still-perfect three-part harmony while approaching the Mystic River Bridge toll booth at about eighty miles an hour. We were returning northward from ascertaining that the bars in the new Faneuil Hall Marketplace were able to keep pace with drinkers of our proficiency.

Cass had just inherited the latest of her father's Cadillac El Dorado castoffs and when we screeched to a halt at the toll booth, she pushed every button in the car except for the one that opened her window. The windshield wipers slapped, the radio antenna went up and down and interior lights flashed. The toll taker was not amused as the line of cars behind us lengthened. We were paralyzed with laughter and the attendant yelled, *"Come on, Girlie...Hurry up!"*

Massachusetts toll booth attendants act like theirs is the toughest job in the world; sticking their hands out for that money, and if (God forbid), they have to make change; they come close to collapsing under the pressure.

Cass flipped the angry man the bird and took off. Looking back out of my open window that no one could manage to close, I saw the idiot jump out of the booth shouting and waving a piece of paper, probably in an attempt to get our plate number. Luckily, we were going much too fast for that.

"For chrissake, all that over a quarter?" Cass fumed. "Asshole'll probably get run over by thirty-five cars."

"I'm just glad they don't give them guns," Molly observed. She was significantly under the influence or she probably would have been a Two Shoes and walked back to pay the toll.

"Cassandra," I observed, "I've noticed over the years that the sight of a uniform doesn't create a spirit of cooperation in you."

She agreed, and Molly offered that it was more than likely an Italian thing.

Cass looked at Molly in her rearview mirror, made a *screw you* motion under her chin and said, "This is an Italian thing, too."

They were such fun.

While Molly had immersed herself in study, Cass and I immersed ourselves in drink and bounced around the working world. I did more bouncing than Cass. This was largely due to the fact that on her second big-girl job at a small printing company, her boss had the bad taste to squeeze her on the butt. She suggested that he try his mother and stormed out. This transgression was reported to her father, who didn't take it well. The following night she overheard Sal on the phone saying "I guess that pile of jewshit won't be grabbing anything for a while."

Cass was then given a desk in the office of her father's construction company, where he could keep an eye on her. Surprisingly, she was soon running the place and doing it well. The guys who worked for her father loved her and she loved them. They were her type. Men who worked with their hands -- and not one of them would have dared to touch any part of her person without permission. Permission was occasionally granted when she was on the outs with Gordo.

In my early working life, I had an incredible series of galloping jackasses for bosses. Eventually I landed at a job at our local daily paper, the saving grace of which was reporting to an insane Englishman named Doyle

Wittingham, who was the day editor. The Daily Union was owned by a family of alleged aristocratic descent, the members of which, thank God, spent a lot of time at their country club and very little at the office.

Doyle had been a commando in the English army during World War II and the word was that he was crazy due to war experiences and his continued use of the bottle to forget them. He was smart and funny and saw the Daily Union owners for the twits that they were. To give them their due, they recognized his talent and gave him far more latitude than he probably deserved. I loved his humor and his English expressions like *will we stop for a jar? (Let's have a drink)* or *is there a hesitation in your step? (Are you hung over?)*

He had a wife and two sons in England and he thought that was a jolly good place for them. His wife threatened a visit now and then, but he'd always manage to sabotage it. We had a platonic affair. He was, after all, almost my father's age. He was quite pleased that the office tongues were busy wagging since I was so much younger than he and everyone thought he was scoring.

The day we learned about Lord Mountbatten's death at the hands of the IRA, we left the office at noon and were not seen again until the next day. Over more than a few "jars," Doyle told me that it was a *good job* that this wasn't twenty years ago or Monty's boys would wipe out the bleedin' IRA. He had served under Mountbatten in North Africa or some terrible place, and no one under his command had anything but respect for their leader. Acting upon a particularly misguided idea, the IRA had blown up Mountbatten's boat, killing him and his young grandson with his daughter watching from the dock.

Princess Margaret, never known for tact, was visiting Chicago at the time, and had made the memorable statement "The Irish, they're pigs" to the face of Mayor Byrne (Irish name). Later it was reported that she had actually said "The

Irish do *jigs*." Pigs or jigs, if the goal of the IRA "soldiers" (ha!) was to prove that they were the world's biggest assholes, they accomplished it. Even Grammy O., who was probably a charter member of the IRA, had conceded that it was a singularly uninspired idea.

Late into the night, Doyle and I discussed the crown's treatment of the Irish over the centuries, like the "First Night" rule, whereby an English nobleman would have the right to deflower an Irish, Scottish or Welsh bride, in keeping with the theory that the fine English input would improve the inferior bloodlines.

"Oh yeah, that was the reason," I observed. We both laughed nastily at that.

Doyle described some of the other favors that the crown had visited upon the Irish: attempting to erase the Irish language, forbidding the Irish to own land, or even dogs, taxing them into starvation. While Doyle admitted to the rudeness of these decrees, I could sense that he needed to be English that night, to be one of them and to hurt for them. The news had also released horrific memories for him.

According to Doyle, commandos are trained to enter an area in advance of the infantry and kill every living creature they encounter. This was their job, and when the war ended, they were expected to shut their mouths and go back to living a proud, guilt-free civilian life. Some of them could do it, some couldn't.

He didn't share the details of what he had been required to do, but I was transfixed by his story of being awakened one night by his friend Charlton, whispering near his ear, *"Doyle, don't move."*

Opening his eyes, his first conscious thought was that there was something dark and warm on his chest. It took a few seconds for him to realize what it was -- a sleeping cobra.

Charlton moved quickly and cocked his rifle, startling the snake into raising its head and he shot it off of Doyle's chest.

I was aghast. "You had the guts to stay still…"

"Guts?" he laughed.

"I was literally petrified. I couldn't move, or I bloody well would have. If I wasn't such a coward I wouldn't be here." His expression changed, he shuddered and shouted, "Wench, more mead!"

"A coward?" I said. "I think not."

**

We all loved my condo. It featured a small kitchen with a brunch bar that opened into the living room via a large pass-through. Above the opening there was a collection of mirrors and neon signs advertising various forms of alcoholic refreshment, which had been appropriated from local establishments by my friend Cassandra.

Below the bar, there was a cabinet containing every kind of libation known to man. Dottie Moscella, who worked as a Northeast Airlines stewardess, frequently brought over bags of "nips" as the beensy bottles of booze were called. On the job, Dottie embraced a modified version of Nonnie's *if they didn't' want you to have it; they wouldn't have left it there* policy. The nips lined the perimeter of the cabinet while larger, more serious bottles stood grandly in the center: Jameson Irish (brought straight from Ireland by Uncle Terry), Chivas Regal, several cognacs, and island rums and tequila from our trips.

There was always a bottle of Stolichnaya in the freezer, to be sipped from pony glasses with a black pepper in the bottom. This assortment of top-shelf spirits was a pretense, since everyone knew that my friends and I would have drunk Red Dog Rotgut from a toilet bowl.

A hall led to a bath and two small bedrooms. One was an actual bedroom and the other a music room with a small pull-out couch upon which a drunken reveler could crash.

The music room's walls were decorated with posters from concerts that I'd attended or wished I had. Three guitars stood grandly side by side: a Jumbo Gibson acoustic, a Fender Telecaster and a beat-up classical -- all of which I could play; an electronic piano which I could barely play; and a drum set that I couldn't play, but enjoyed banging on.

It seemed that the musical genetic contributions of Delchi Labastiani had been equally divided between Doc and me. Doc could play the drums and the concertina (bequeathed by some ancestral Labastiani to my father.) The older two archangels mocked us for our efforts, but outside of the house bragged about our talent and sometimes commanded that we play *Wipeout* for their friends, who seemed suitably impressed.

Prominently featured in my living room was my collection of "Bobs." Molly, Cass and I had visited a number of islands during the late sixties and early seventies. Dottie would alert us to unfilled charters and we could fly cheaply, leaving us plenty of entertainment money.

Ceramic figurines of black native children with huge heads that were attached to a spring were a favorite island souvenir of that era. Bermuda Bob, Bahama Bob, and Bimini Bob were lined up on top of my bookcase. I enjoyed pushing their heads down and watching them bounce up and down; forcing them to agree with whatever I had just said. A picture of Cass, Molly and me from each trip was displayed next to the appropriate Bob.

There had once been an Acapulco Bob, but Phineas took a dislike to him and pushed him off of the bookcase, causing his oversized head to split in two. I suspect that the cat is a fan of alliteration and found the inclusion of *Acapulco Bob* unacceptable.

**

Of the six bars on "my" wharf, The Frig was our favorite, due to its proximity to my condo and the fact that it had both drink and cheap eats. Molly was the only one of us who could cook but she preferred not to do so, since her father had put her to work flipping burgers at the *Fife and Drum* when she was six.

The name of the Frig was actually The Outrigger, which is some contraption of a boating accessory nature. We started calling it the Outfrigger and then shortened it to just the Frig.

Walter Kodie had started working there in high school, cleaning up and stocking. Eventually, he became a bartender and when the owners decided that they preferred a quiet Florida escape to payment of taxes, they made it easy for him to buy it.

The Frig was flanked on its right by Knotical Treasures, Purveyors of Seafaring Merchandise, and on its left by the Sadie Madison Doll Shop. In both cases, the fare ran from true treasures to worthless junk. Sadie Madison, (nee Ethel Braughenstein) who had run her shop for decades, lived by the rule that you could fool some of the people some of the time and a tourist all of the time. Ethel was inclined toward the sharing of whispered confidences like "It's rumored that this doll belonged to Louisa May Alcott when she was a child." She knew these rumors well, having been the one who started them.

She dressed plainly and wore no makeup at the shop, but Cass had once seen her at the Top of the Hub Restaurant dressed to the nines and sporting diamond rings on nearly all of her fingers.

**

"Keep Calm and Carry On," Doyle bellowed the first time he entered the Frig.

"Who's this nut? Cass asked, twirling her swizzle stick in her gin and tonic.

"That nut, I'm pleased to announce, is my boss at the Daily Union and you shouldn't be drinking gin. It makes you tell lies."

"This isn't gin."

"See what I mean? I can smell the juniper from here. It's cuckoo juice."

Because she was indeed lying and didn't want to know what juniper was, she ignored me and stood up. "Kit's Boss," she hollered, "Over here!"

Doyle marched straight to our table, turned a chair around backward and sat down on it like he owned the place.

"Barkeep, another round for these two prostitutes I've hired, if you please," he shouted to Walter, who sneered at all of us.

"Uh-oh, he's Alfred tonight," Cass observed. "You'd think even Alfred would love us for the money we drop in here. He could buy a new house."

"Or a personality," I offered.

Cass shook her head. "Let's not go crazy."

A while later, upon returning from the powder room, I sat down to the following exchange.

"So," Doyle said, "an R.C. believes…"

"What's an R.C?" Cass interrupted.

"Roman Catholic."

"Go on."

"Your RC's believe that un-baptized babies go to some appalling place called Limbo."

"That's right...where they're forced to dance under a stick for all of eternity," Cass informed him. "I heard that on TV."

"Serves them bloody well right...dying without arranging a proper baptism."

They guffawed loudly and beamed at each other, admiring their mutual irreverence. I should have guessed that two rabble-rousers like these two would adore each other.

When I left at eleven, it was clear that they were both enchanted. I went home and went to bed only to be awakened by the insistent ringing of my doorbell at one o'clock in the morning. Donning my bunny slippers, I shuffled to the door, feeling pretty certain of who was doing the ringing.

I looked through the peephole and a huge blue eye stared back.

"Open the door, for chrissake. It's freezing out here," Cass commanded.

Cass and Doyle tumbled into the hall and Cass said, "We need a drink."

"I seriously doubt that," I said.

"Let's rephrase," Doyle said. "We *demahnd* a drink. Or we make one room of this place." He took a seat at the brunch bar.

"Fair enough...vodka, scotch or rye?" I offered.

"Yes," they both answered, and went into fits of laughter.

It was going to be a long night.

**

As investigative reporter, I'm not without worth. I've learned that the way to get people to talk to you is to start with their favorite subject – them.

However, it's also been my experience that the more willing a person is to talk, the fewer facts they have. People with bad information will spill their guts while those who actually know the score will tell you to get off their property or they'll shoot you.

Although I make money from newspapers, I never read one. They're full of inaccuracies and biased blather. There's no such thing as an objective report. Follow the thread and someone is being served, most likely a deep-pocketed advertiser or politician. Each day, in the way of atonement, back pages are filled with small-print retractions of the lies that were printed in bold the day before. I should write only fiction, where lies are not only permitted, but required.

**

At Christmas time, Doyle took me and my dear friends Molly and Cassandra to Chinatown for what he called the Feast of a Thousand Drinks, which we were pretty sure he made up, but we weren't the kind of people to question such a ritual. Food was served right at the bar in the no-name establishment he had found and we never had to leave our seats. Or eat the food, for that matter.

After Doyle's checking with each of us to see if we thought Chinese people looked like grasshoppers and getting validation on the point (three times) and we had worked the HOW LONG IS A CHINAMAN thing to death, we somehow began a spirited comparison of Irish and Italian Catholics. Doyle was fascinated by Catholicism, for reasons known only to him. We then moved on to the general differences between Irish and Italian people.

This discussion was so raucous that nearby patrons began to join in. An Italian woman said that her father told her that an Italian couldn't become an alcoholic. You had to be Irish. A guy from Southie, who was standing at the bar drinking, offered that his Irish-Italian family referred to themselves as members of the Harpanwop Tribe.

Amid the hilarity, Doyle turned to me and said, "There's a bloody good chance that I won't remember this tomorrow so I'm asking you now. Write it up and we'll print it."

Surprised, I countered, "There's also a bloody good chance that we won't find it hilarious tomorrow."

Doyle winked. "Methinks we will."

The next day, with a hesitation in my step, I wrote the article.

**

THE HARPANWOP CONUNDRUM

Beliefs of Tribal Members

As Told to K. Labastiani

Shouldn't Irish ice and Italian fire create a balanced human being?

WHY THEY DON'T:

1.) Church – *Irish:* A place you go to atone for your sins. *Italian:* A place to go to see your relatives. Guilt doesn't work with Italians.

2.) Sending Offspring to Join a Convent/Seminary – *Irish:* Points off of guilt tally and there would be no sex. *Italian:* Why go anywhere that you can't have sex?

3.) Gravy - *Irish:* Brown substance derived from the fat of meats. It is poured over meat, potatoes and occasionally someone's head. *Italian:* Red sauce that must always be heating on stovetop. It is poured over every food but oatmeal. In most tribal homes, what is ladled onto pasta is Irish-Italian Gravy/Sauce.

4.) Mode of Expression – *Irish:* "There's no heat to speak of in this room today." *Italian:* "'Ay! I'm freezin' my lugatz off."

There were letters. Some readers were outraged by the words *harp* and *wop* but in the main, responses not only verified all that the article had put forth, but offered a number of Italian/Irish incompatibility points that we had missed.

Doyle asked me if I wanted to write a follow-up and I thought that would be much more fun than sitting in a town meeting in front of a table full of posers with petty power syndrome yammering ad nauseam about whether or not someone could put up a goddamned fence, while I pictured all of their heads exploding, one by one.

**

CHAPTER

Bamberg, Germany

Death at the stake was designed for maximum suffering. Its victim didn't burst into flames and instantly die. It was an unhurried process wherein the sufferer roasted slowly, making for ever-increasing pain and a lengthy presentation of agony for the crowd. Executions took place behind All Saints Prison, where the animals were kept. It was as foul a murder place as the righteous clergy could arrange.

Anke's face no longer looked human. Her right eye was bruised to a dark purple, several times its normal size and swollen shut.

Two guards dragged her battered body through the cheering crowd. People spit at her through rotting teeth and a child in filthy rags ran up and flung dried animal dung at her as she was being tethered to the goats' stake.

Who would expose a child to this... she thought and prayed that little Emil had reached Magda's cottage safely.

She turned her head slowly and surveyed the crowd with her good eye. The prince bishop was present, standing partly in shadow under a large lean-to. Her good eye found him and she smiled at him. Looking at her face unnerved him, but he couldn't manage to look away.

While the kindling sticks that were piled around her feet were being ignited with torches brandished by the eager guards, Anke steadily held the gaze of the bishop. Her lips never moved, but he clearly heard her voice and it said *this is what your god wants?"*

He visibly started and one of his aides leaned toward him questioningly, but the bishop appeared mesmerized.

The crowd continued to throw debris and rocks at the prisoner. When a particularly large stone grazed her shoulder forcefully, she closed her good eye, still smiling. There was no pain.

The kindling wood began to smoke and as a grey film began to obscure her face, the prince bishop shifted his weight from one foot to the other, with a mystified expression. Looking more and more puzzled, he hopped on his left foot and then his right. His entourage began to close ranks around him as he kicked off his leather slippers and began to shout. Another priest grabbed the cleric's arm but he shook loose and began to run toward the animals' water trough. To the amazement of all present, he started to tear the silk robes from his body and throw the sacred vestment pieces on the ground.

The mob forgot Anke, and gaped at Schelt as he threw himself, dazed and nearly naked, into the water trough. He screamed as the skin on his feet and lower legs reddened, blistered and finally sloughed off in large pieces into the water.

Anke's smile remained, although she no longer occupied her ruined body. The lack of vocalized agony was disappointing to the crowd, who had rallied all of their hate for the execution and planned to enjoy the suffering of the witch.

The bishop fainted; his entire body scalded and blackened by something that no one could explain. He was taken to his palatial home where he eventually regained consciousness and alternately cursed God and begged anyone who would listen to find a wise woman to heal him.

"Delirious from the pain," his subordinates explained to each other nervously, more appalled by the request for a wise woman than by his cursing of God.

He lived, ranting, for three days and died in agony.

**

CHAPTER

Port Locke, Massachusetts

Cass's obsession with style and my lack of interest in it provided her with endless entertainment. She was particularly amused by my investigative reporter raincoat, which she had named Lois, after Lois Lane, Clark Kent's gal pal reporter. Lois had begun life as a highly practical all-season trench coat. She was an uninspired hue of taupe and contained an equally boring beige woolen zip-out lining, enabling me, to Cass's disgust, to sport her during all phases of the variable New England weather. Cass had about twenty raincoats, ranging from a pink vinyl number to a chic black and white herringbone and everything in between. Not a one was taupe.

Having once too often left a purse or pocketbook containing meaningful things in a bar or forgotten location, I had made yet another responsible decision: to travel light and carry necessities in the pockets of Lois, despite this causing the coat to weigh as much as I did and hang off of my shoulders at an unnatural angle, either to the left or right, depending on which pocket contained the most weight. It worked for me, if not for Cass.

**

Due to the fact that we were guzzling coffee at Dunkin' Donuts rather than going to church, Cass and I missed the one mass we would have enjoyed. On a Sunday morning a few years after graduation, it was announced from the pulpit that former Immaculata teacher Sister Finn Faith had gone to eternal rest.

The proclamation was made by a visiting priest who hadn't had the pleasure of knowing the nun and therefore had made the mistake of asking all present to remember her lovingly in their prayers.

At first there were a few snickers, followed by giggles. In the end there were belly laughs, applause and even a few whistles. The priest was bewildered. He smiled uncertainly and continued reading the weekly bulletin, but could barely be heard above the celebrating.

My brother Doc came into Dunkin' Donuts smiling and bearing the news. He ordered coffee and we all toasted Sister Fishface. He led with "May she rot in hell."

"Gone to God and he can have her," I added.

"I hope it was painful," Cass said, through narrowed eyes.

Even the counterman joined in with "God, I hated her. She nearly knocked out one of my front teeth because she caught me with a yoyo. You woulda thought it was a switchblade."

In parochial school doctrine, having a yoyo was sinful and whacking a child in the mouth was not.

**

It was around this time that Cass and I had invented our own religion. My cousin Nora, who was in our graduating class, got as much of a bang out of Cass as I did, and we were both invited to her wedding a year after graduation. She had the good taste to buck her family and marry OUTSIDE OF THE FAITH in a lovely little white Protestant church overlooking the sea. Cass and I stared in wonder at the bright white walls and simplicity of the whole thing. *Where was the gore...the suffering ... the guilt?*

We vowed that thereafter we would be known as Episcatarians, which was our word for all Protestant denominations. It pertains to any church that you could belong to but didn't have to bother to actually attend. Molly also joined the movement as we had always been envious of our Protestant friends who didn't have to go to church under threat of eternal damnation. Some of their churches even suspended services in the summer. Grammy O. was appalled by the fact that a *Prod* family would change religions if they happened to move closer to a different denomination church. She would sputter, *"To them, it's like changing their knickers!"*

**

Later that night, at Cass's house, I was eyeing the plain olive wood cross hanging over her bed. Her aunt Angie had recently brought it back from Rome.

"Is this due to your deep belief in Christianity or in vampires?"

"Oh, vampires," she replied quickly.

"That's what I figured. Besides, it looks more Episcatarian without a body attached. More fun."

Cass was suddenly serious, which always threw me off balance. She looked away from her much-loved three-paneled mirror and said, "I doubt that it was fun for him to have his own people turn on him, torture and kill him."

I was uncharacteristically speechless. Then she shook her head as if coming out of a dream and said, "Let's go to Barnaby's for last call."

We did.

**

I met Cass at the Frig at high noon, as prior-to-noon drinking was for those with a problem. She was sitting at the bar, sipping on a Bloody Mary.

"What would you do if you knew you only had a month to live?" she demanded as I took my customary stool.

"Kill all the mimes," I replied, after ordering a Blow the Man Down; a nautical specialty of the house that invited verbal variations too obvious to mention.

Cass raised her left eyebrow.

"They creep me out," I explained.

Cass had raised non sequiturs to an art form and her response to that was, "I'm sick of all this bi-centennial crap. Tomorrow's the fourth of July."

"And today is the third," I observed. "So what?"

"So, should we attend my family's Romanesque-eat-until-you-projectile-vomit-party?"

"Your beau's not around?"

She smirked. "No, he's at his daddy's camp killing fish and spitting on the floor."

Gordo's father often entertained his clients with a weekend getaway at their New Hampshire lake house. Gordo the Turd was always assigned the task of operating the boat since the old man and clients were always stinking drunk. Gordo said that most of them would have screamed for their mothers if they had to take a squirming fish off of a hook. Luckily, they never caught any.

"In that case, perhaps you prefer my family's Irish get-drunk-and-make-people-cry funfest. I leave it to you."

"Remember the year Uncle Terry got pissed and zoomed out of the driveway with your cousin's new GTO attached to his bumper?"

"That was memorable," I chuckled.

Cass rose suddenly and headed for the powder room since she hadn't seen her face or attire for ten minutes. During her absence I stirred my cocktail and recalled other alcohol-fueled extravaganzas staged by my family members on various holidays.

They had gotten worse over the years. It was always a toss-up to see which of the aunties or uncles would lose their minds first and start picking at emotional scabs until somebody bled. It was very trying to keep steering them away from any subject that would make them get nasty, which was any subject at all, since getting nasty was the goal. Even if the one you were attending to didn't take center stage, it was quite taxing to agree with things you didn't agree with and generally babysit the so-called adults. And, if they didn't start trouble, you were always on high alert waiting for it. It was tedious and altogether unfair. I decided to forego the pleasure of their company this year and do something constructive, like drink with my friends.

"Do you want some sustenance?" I asked Cass upon her return. Whenever I suggested food, Cass would look at me blankly and I would remind her, "You know, that stuff you put in your tummy so that you can drink more?"

Most often she would pass, while Molly and I were not averse to slurping the Frig's New England clam chowder, which Walt/Alfred bought from the Boston Atlantic Fish Pier Company every day. It was authentic and tasty, especially when accompanied by the fresh rolls he had delivered daily by the Apollo Agora Bakery. Molly said she liked to eat soup because it was easier to throw up.

** **

As expected, the Black Rose had a fit and fell in it over my Harpanwop column. "You make the Irish sound like a bunch of stiffs," she hissed at me over dinner.

"It's just always amused me that the Irish and Italians look down on each other with equal disdain," I answered.

To wit, my Irish relatives would never grasp that the Italians saw them as drunken wastrels who spend all their money on booze and would rather fight than fornicate. (It's been pointed out often that only a group of Irish people can dance frantically and have not one pelvis in motion.)

The Italians would have been just as amazed to find that the Irish thought of them as swarthy, undisciplined cheats who were too lazy or stupid to be anything other than criminals. My mother's father's comments on her engagement to an Italian were "To be happy, they (Italians) have to be doing something illegal," followed up by "and they always go after the white girls."

As these high-minded concepts were being flung around the dinner table, Raphael observed, "The funny part is they're both right."

"And they're both wrong," Doc added, and for once was not corrected by Rafe...or anyone else.

Rafe then quoted, "Never trust a generalization; including this one."

"Right," Doc agreed. "Dad isn't a crook and Mom isn't a drunk, but generalizations get started for a reason."

Michael looked at Raphael to see if he would correct Doc and when he didn't, Michael offered, "And then there's Uncle Slug."

Dad chuckled heartily.

"And Cousin Angelo, who's doing three to five," I contributed.

The Black Rose also chuckled.

Since I didn't get shot down for once, I ventured into prickly territory.

"You know, every time I mention something that anyone in this family doesn't want to discuss, I'm told to go peel the potatoes, so it's no wonder all the Irish left the country during the potato famine. Otherwise, they may have had to talk to each other."

There was an atypical moment of silence.

"Well, the lack of *food* may have had something to do with it," the Black Rose sniffed, and then looked at me thoughtfully. I told myself, *if she tells me to go peel potatoes, I'll run away from home.* But she didn't. One thing I have to give the BR is that although she was always up for an argument, and was pretty good at it, in the end she seemed to consider what other people had to say. Maybe she was just working on a better argument for the next time the given subject arose.

The Italian/Irish marital combination that's so prevalent in Boston tends to make for smart and good-looking offspring. My brothers are handsome and while I wouldn't win any pageants, I'm not without admirers. We all did well scholastically. Molly's family respected education above all and Cassie's thought it was a waste of money. My family compromised by believing that only male children should be educated.

Since Cass was a full-blooded Italian and Molly as Irish as the gin blossoms on my uncle's nose, they both referred to me as a half-breed. I was a thick Mick to Cass and a dumb grease-ball to Molly whenever I displeased one of them.

**

It was late on a Friday afternoon when I arrived at the Frig, and Cass was holding court with a group of Syrian sailors.

The tall ships were in, containing tall sailors. Her enthusiasm and high coloring indicated that she had been there a while. Beginning the weekend early was one of the perks of working for Dad.

Cass spotted me and immediately had all of the Syrian sailors yelling, "Kit, Kit, Kit!" They were all pretty happy to see me. That's the great thing about drinking people – they don't have to know you to be moved to tears at the sight of you.

I joined them, anxious to bring my level of joy up to theirs. A round of drinks appeared and Cass pushed one of the three Monsoons that sat in front of her toward me. I picked up the drink and toasted "Death and Destruction" to the smiling Syrians, who vigorously agreed and we all clinked glasses and drank.

The vodka and fruit juices slid soothingly down my throat. *"Ahhh..."* I said, and meant it. I looked around the place. "Where's Gordo?" I asked. He was usually present at the Frig on Fridays.

Cass looked at me questioningly. "Who?"

That was a conversation that was headed nowhere, so I turned my attention to the sailor on my right.

"Nice uniform." They did look pretty spiffy in their white uniforms that contrasted their dark skin. He looked over at Cass and said "Yes, yes, yes," but I don't think we were talking about the same thing.

We ducked out on the sailors about nine and it was to be the memorable night that Cass, quite literally, crashed at my condo. I had encouraged her to leave the Cadillac safely parked in the wharf's public lot but she wanted the car in sight on the morrow, probably so she'd know where the hell it was. I was her unwilling passenger as she whipped the huge car out of the lot, around the corner and into the entrance to my condo complex parking lot. It was a twelve-second ride.

The Caddy blasted down the middle of the parking lot. Regrettably, one of her anthems from our high school days, *I Get Around* by the Beach Boys began playing on the car radio and she screamed and started fiddling with the tuning knob. Cass neglected to slow down as we approached my building and with the radio volume having reached the perfect million-decibel level, we proceeded to crash into the building.

Another good thing about drinking people is that this event might have embarrassed a sober person, whereas Cass was merely confused and rather annoyed by the fact that we were sitting in her car, which was, in turn, sitting in the living room of my neighbors, the Twinnie Winnies.

The story told was that when the twin sisters were born a hundred years ago, they were identical, and since no one could tell them apart, they were both named Winnie. The family avoided confusion and all of their lives, the LaMarche twins called each other by the same name. They were French and Uncle Slug said that explained it.

They were now old women and were both yelling – one into the kitchen phone and the other at us.

I looked over at Cass and asked, "Are you hurt?"

She shook her head. "No. Are you?"

"I don't think so. Are they?" I asked, nodding toward the sisters.

"If they were hurt, they'd be dead."

There was momentary silence and then we both started to laugh and were nearing hysterics when we heard sirens.

"Shit, we gotta get outta here," Cass whispered to me and frantically tried to start the car, which wasn't happening. It wasn't clear why, since the car was in much better shape than the living room. Condo walls had little to no chance against a '74 Caddy.

I opened the car door and asked the Twinnie Winnies if they'd like to come to my condo for a cup of coffee and they both looked at me like I had asked them to go to the moon in a hot air balloon.

Cass exited the vehicle and assured them that we would simply call a tow truck and all would be well. Blue lights began to flash outside and the rest of that evening isn't a memory that I can't entirely retrieve, which is probably just as well.

**

CHAPTER

Mannington, Massachusetts

My ascent through the ranks of the Daily Union was meaningless, but swift. I began in the Circulation Department where my life consisted of listening to subscribers express their disapproval of having their morning news land in a tree, on the roof or not show up at all. I learned that news carriers of all ages have a tendency to resign from their positions without informing anyone. It got old immediately.

Next I was assigned to the Production Department, so named because it was indeed a production to get them to do anything. Their group had been hit the hardest by the big bad computers (one hundred employees had been axed) and those who were left remembered the good old days too well. Those who didn't remember them and tried to do a satisfactory job would be driven out, bleeding from the ears. They still had a strong union and wouldn't hand you a pencil if it wasn't in their job description. I loathed everyone in the department and the feeling was mutual.

Most news writers begin in the trade by writing obituaries, but on my first day in that capacity, just for drill, I had modified the obit template by filling in *Larry, Moe* and *Curly* as the names of the next of kin, and it was nearly printed for all of that day's dearly departed. Luckily, it was caught by a proofreader who corrected it. I was then promoted to reporter. If I had burned down the building, I might have been made editor-in-chief.

Finally landing in the News Department, I got to cover exciting events like the grand opening of a button shop, numbingly tedious city council meetings and anything else that someone with a byline wouldn't vomit upon.

Occasionally they let me pen an editorial, which invariably led to outrage and I'd end up back at the council meetings.

Of the fifty-seven people who worked at the Daily Union, there were three that I liked. One was Doyle and another was Ellie Maplewaithe, who was a researcher, librarian and an all-around smarty pants. She was witty like Doyle but a lot less crazy. Trivial Pursuit was popular then and it was played by the staff at lunchtime. Ellie had never had a question that she couldn't answer. The other players thought they had her once and it turned out that the answer on the card was wrong and Ellie was right.

The paper's administration stuck her in a crappy little corner office and paid her next to nothing, but would trot her out whenever a dignitary or politician visited, thereby demonstrating that their staff members were the finest specimens of class and superior intelligence.

The third name on my short list was Maryelle Day from Louisiana. She was a big black woman who came in late in the afternoons to help bundle the papers. I always looked forward to her arrival. She'd ask a question and whatever you replied, she'd say "*'Shonuff!'*" with infectious enthusiasm, big dimples and perfect teeth.

She and her husband Booker were known to go missing every now and then. After one of her excused two-day "mourning" absences, Doyle pointed out to her that it was about the fourth grandmother she'd lost that year. She replied, *"Yuh, well, we all ve'y close."* He collapsed laughing and loved her from that day on.

The offices were located in the east wing of a historic building called the Croft Mercantile, which utilized a pneumatic tube system that was used to send documents from one floor to another, before computers became commonplace. The plastic tube was almost always stuck in the chute somewhere between two of the four floors. When this occurred, one of the sixth-floor personnel would be asked to drop a two-inch steel ball bearing down the chute in an effort to free the jam. When the endeavor worked, the tube, propelled by the weight of the bearing, would blast out of the first floor chute at warp speed and the bearing would break your foot if you were dumb enough to stand there.

When there was an obituary or memoriam photo to be printed, the deceased's loved one would beg the staff to *take extra special care...it's one of a kind...the only picture we have...* When the grieving had departed, one of us would roll up the precious photo and stick it in the magical mystery tube, often never to be seen again.

The Layout Group's response to complaints was *"And that's the only picture they have of their loved one...one picture?"* They had a point, but it didn't console the bereaved whatsoever.

**

CHAPTER

Port Locke, Massachusetts

Perched atop the Outrigger's porch roof, and completely out of keeping with its nautical theme and surroundings, was a black 19th century buggy harnessed to a stuffed white horse and containing (weather permitting) two stuffed dummies who greatly resembled Sonny and Cher.

On a few occasions Cass and Gordo had decided that nothing would entertain them so much as to climb atop said decoration, replace the dummies with themselves (also dummies) and suddenly come to life, to the great consternation of whoever happened to look up at them. It was an authentic old buggy and for some reason, the prize possession of Walt/Alfred Kobie. I arrived one evening to find him addressing the establishment's first couple thus:

"Get offa there you friggin' idiots or I'll call the cops!"

"Yeehaw!" was the enthusiastic reply from above. Cass, no doubt influenced by her good friend Captain Morgan, was busy whipping the stuffed horse while singing *Baby Don't Go* at the top of her lungs. This lyrical entreaty went unheeded by Gordon Coelridge Wells, who walked to the end of the porch roof and began to urinate. Walt/Alfred was scandalized and went inside to call the police.

I thought this a good point at which to intervene and shouted, *"Free drinks at the Crown Sloop. Come down!"*

They did, and I knew it was not the word *free* but the word *drinks* that had caused them to cooperate and thereby evade police action. When the cruiser pulled into the wharf, we were five bars down and as the officers were not quite as outraged as Walt about this transgression, there was no manhunt mounted.

**

CHAPTER

Bamberg, Germany

Frederich sat on a high rock and watched the sickening tableau below. He couldn't cry or shout. His beloved Anke was being led through a jeering crowd and would soon die an excruciating death at the hands of *churchmen.*

He spat on the ground watching the ceremonious arrival of the prince bishop and his entourage of priests, dressed in their grand silk robes. He looked down at his coarse clothing and his hands, hardened and scarred from working the farm. These sniveling clerics had never done an honest day's work, and now they were taking one of the few things in his life that was beautiful. She was better than all of them and they knew it and feared her. They justified lies and murders in the name of their god, and he could do nothing to stop them.

As a column of grey smoke began to rise, Frederich turned away, fell to his knees and prayed that there was a god waiting for all of them.

**

CHAPTER

Port Locke, Massachusetts

It was just after closing and Cass was somewhat unsteadily climbing the back stairs of the Frig. She was just drunk enough to think that visiting the rooftop horse and carriage was an excellent plan. She and Gordo had enjoyed many good times there.

He was a few steps behind her, telling her to slow down, but she ignored him. Gaining access to the roof, she hurried to the stuffed dummies and removed them from their seat. She hid beneath the bench seat and jumped up and yelled "Gotcha!" when he got close to the carriage.

"Jesus Christ!" he swore at her and nearly dropped the bottle of peppermint schnapps that he had in his hand. "Are you nuts?"

"Don't be such a wimp!" she laughed, and plunked down on the red cushioned seat.

He sat down beside her and put his arm around her shoulder. She shrugged it away.

"What's your problem?" he growled.

"I don't have a problem," she answered pleasantly. She grabbed the whip and snapped it over the stuffed horse's hind quarter.

His eyes narrowed and he glared at her with an anger that might have frightened her if she had noticed. He opened the bottle and passed it under her nose. When she reached for it, he pulled it away, with an evil grin.

"Asshole," she said, and stood up to leave.

"Oh, please don't play hard to get. I know better."

He grabbed her hand and coaxed, "Come on, have a drink."

The invitation inspired forgiveness and she sat back down. She took a swallow from the bottle. It tasted minty and she said, "This is great if you like mouthwash." She took another healthy swig, nonetheless.

When she handed back the bottle, he screwed the top back on and reached for her. She attempted to push him away and he slapped her in the face. When the shock wore off, she said, "That was a mistake, dickhead," rubbing her cheek and standing up to leave.

"Sit the fuck down," he commanded, pushing her back onto the seat. She was beginning to feel trapped and didn't like it.

"No, I won't sit the fuck anywhere." She stood up again and tried to climb past him.

He jumped up and shoved her out of the cart. Landing painfully on the gravel roof, she was momentarily paralyzed, but then started to yell, knowing that there was usually a police presence on the wharf at that hour.

He was instantly on top of her. Through clenched teeth he whispered, "I'm warning you. Shut up!" He covered her mouth with his right hand and pressed on her throat with the left. She bit his hand and when he pulled it away she screamed again, hoping to bring him back to reality. Instead, he put both hands around her neck and began to squeeze.

**

Doyle called at ten a.m. and suggested meeting for an early lunch. Say, around noon, just after the "public houses" opened. I hadn't heard from Cassie but I never called her in the morning, as it could bring the family's attention to the fact that she had failed to come home the night before. I knew that I'd encounter her eventually at one of our favored establishments.

It was raining as I approached the Frig and I had to navigate around puddles for the sake of the absurdly expensive green suede boots that Cass had talked me into buying. I looked up briefly before I ducked under the overhanging porch roof and had a sense that something was out of place. I stopped, backed up and looked up again at the horse and buggy. The rain had started suddenly and the dummy dolls had not been taken inside. The Sonny doll was in his usual place, but in place of Cher there was a different figure – a figure with a face that I recognized in spite of the black and blue flesh and vacant eyes. It wasn't Cher and it wasn't a doll.

It was Cass.

**

Doyle said later that he had heard me frantically shouting Cass's name and he and two other Frig patrons had run out to find me trying to climb up one of the support posts to the porch roof. He pulled me down and I remember pointing at the roof. When he looked up, his face filled with horror. More people assembled and someone was yelling, *"Call the cops!"* I shouted for someone to call an ambulance but even as I said it, I knew it was too late.

What offended me most was the rain falling on her face. I wanted someone to cover her face…not to see that her bloodied eyes didn't blink against the rain.

**

CHAPTER

Bamberg, Germany

The death of Prince Bishop Schelt had raised the level of hysteria and determination of the people to rid the region of its witches and other blasphemers.

Emil was crouching behind the cottage, patting a little white dog, when Frederich spied him. As he neared the boy, he whistled to him and dropped the bundle of apples that he had just picked.

Emil ran to his uncle, who picked him up and swung him high in the air. As he did so, Frederich was struck by the boy's resemblance to Anke and he felt a stabbing pain in the pit of his stomach.

The boy laughed happily while airborne and when his feet were again on solid ground, he grew suddenly sober.

"Where is my mother?" he asked seriously.

Magda leaned out of the open window as Frederich squatted in front of the boy.

"Your mother has gone with the angels" he said softly.

The boy looked shocked.

"Why? Why did she leave me?"

Magda could almost hear Frederich's heart break, along with her own.

"She didn't want to leave you, Emil. I promise you, she had no choice. Aunt Magda and I will always take care of you."

Frederich tried not to let his hatred for the forces that had ended Anke's life enter into the conversation, and he made a sudden decision. Looking steadily into the boy's eyes he said, "I'm not your uncle, Emil. I'm your father."

Hearing this, Magda covered her face with both hands and sobbed.

CHAPTER

Port Locke, Massachusetts

John Paul Prescott was an overweight inbred Yankee with enough family juice to keep him getting promoted rather than fired from every job he'd ever had.

When he was promoted to lieutenant of police over several other crime-fighters who actually had brains, the station house personnel were not feeling particularly congratulatory. It was in this period that he had come by his nickname.

One evening, two of his admiring coworkers had broken a couple of beer bottles in front of the rear wheels of his car and he hadn't gone a mile toward home when both rear tires went flat. It was eleven-thirty at night when he radioed to the police dispatcher for assistance.

After waiting for half an hour, he took matters into his own incompetent hands and jacked up the back of the car. He was underneath the car, in front of the back wheels, when the improperly secured jack fell and the car dropped down, rolled over him and halfway down the hill just as a road assistance vehicle with two fellow officers turned the corner. Said officers hastened to his rescue as soon as they finished laughing themselves sick. "Speed Bump" it was, that night and forever.

The very same Speed Bump had just folded his chubby arms on the table and leaned toward me like he was my dearest friend. He had dragged a chair over to our table at the Frig and plunked his fat butt on it with an unattractive grunt.

"So...it looks like your friend ran into the wrong ride home," he drawled pleasantly.

I shook my head in disbelief and Doyle pushed his chair back from the table, ready to rumble.

"Perhaps at this bleedin' time…" he began.

Speed Bump thundered, "She found the body, and I have to question her!"

Doyle made a move toward him but I took hold of his arm and said, "Would you get me a Wild Turkey please?"

He glared at the officer and then turned to me. "A shot?"

"No, a bottle."

Doyle turned one more murderous look on Prescott and stomped off to the bar.

"And where were you last night?" Speedy asked cordially.

"Me?"

I was startled and then a little anxious when I couldn't immediately think of where I had been the night before. After some concentration, I said, "Oh, at a family gathering." I had, along with my cousins, toasted an upcoming birth repeatedly and my memory of the evening was somewhat vague.

He sneered, probably due to his affection for my delightful brothers, who had once chain-locked his bike to one of the cows on the Rooftop Steak House's front lawn and told everyone that the cow was Prescott's new girl friend.

"A baby shower, I elaborated, "for my cousin's wife."

"You didn't see her?" he asked

"My cousin's wife?"

"No," he snapped. "I meant the victim."

"The *victim* has a name and I just told you I was at a stupid shower." I was beyond outraged by having to discuss anything about Cass's death with this idiot.

"OK, then. Where was her boyfriend?"

"How would I know?"

"I thought all of you were…umm…close," he said, with a knowing look that suggested we had nightly Roman orgies to which he wasn't invited.

"I can assure you that Gordo doesn't report to me," I said, thinking *and he won't report to you either, you stupid fat fuck.*

He sneered again. He hated Gordon Wells as much as he hated my brothers. Maybe he just hated anyone who wasn't fat.

"They fight a lot, right?" he asked, clearly enjoying himself.

Although this was the understatement of the century, it was not his business, and I was in no mood to justify anything. I was beginning to understand why people told me to beat it when I stuck my reporter's nose where it didn't belong.

"Like any couple," I answered. "No more, no less."

"Well, I'll find out where Mr. Wells was."

"Go right ahead, but he'd never hurt Cass. Maybe you could try catching whoever actually did." I wanted to cry but I would not be doing so in front of Speed Bump Prescott.

"Well, I've heard some of their brawls were pretty wild."

It was my turn to sneer. "I think you may be overrating the drama in our drab little lives," I said and stood up.

I held up my right hand in a Girl Scout salute and said, "I promise not to leave town," just as Doyle returned with two glasses and a bottle of Wild Turkey. Walt had given it to him "on the house." We sought better company (our own) at a different table. We stared at each other in shock for a few minutes, and then Doyle cracked the seal on the bottle.

**

CHAPTER

Port Locke, Massachusetts

"Uncle Slug, this is Kit."

"Hey, are you doing okay?"

"Yuh...I just wanted to ask you if you could maybe use your contacts to find out if there's anything new about...Cassie's case. That Prescott nitwit seems to be in charge, which I find alarming."

He snorted. "Damn skippy. I'll make a call. Are you sure you're okay?"

"I'm fine. I just don't want this to turn into one of the greater New England unsolved crimes."

"It won't if I can help it."

"Thanks...and let me know what you find out?"

**

Later that day, Uncle Slug called to say that one of his pals had been told that a matchbook from the Korral Klub was found on the roof of the Frig when they removed the buggy. One of Speed Bump's minions had picked it up and started to light a smoke when another officer pointed out that it might be evidence. The Korral was a strip joint in the downtown part of Mannington, a city that bordered Port Locke.

"Can they get a fingerprint from it?" I asked.

"They could if they could find it."

"What?"

"It's missing."

"No…are they really that incompetent?"

"Since I retired? Yes."

**

CHAPTER

Mannington, Massachusetts

Feeling quite silly and conspicuous, I approached the Korral Klub at high noon. It was not a place that drew female clientele, but it was the only lead in a murder case that was destined to be woefully mismanaged. The more degenerate of the guys I worked with at the paper had spoken fondly of the lunch-hour shows.

Once inside the door, while I tried to make myself invisible, I was assailed by the combined odor of industrial disinfectant, beer and cigarette smoke. There may have one or two other aromas on which I preferred not to dwell. The place was probably not pretty at night, but in the harsh light of day (what there was of it), the seediness couldn't be disguised.

I Shot the Sheriff was blaring from a fuzzy sound system that made up in volume what it lacked in quality. A blonde dancer was performing in the middle on a horseshow-shaped stage, sporting only a pink boa around her neck and matching gun-belt around her waist. She mimed shooting at the guys at the bar who cheered her on. A pink marquis card above her head spelled out her name -- *Feather Canyon* in silver glitter.

I slid into a chair against the back wall and a Hispanic waitress approached me warily and said, "Help jou?"

"Uh, Coke?" She seemed confused and to clarify that I meant the beverage and not the drug, I motioned a drinking gesture. She nodded and returned with a Coke on the rocks in a glass that was never going to touch my lips. I asked for a straw, which she produced from her apron pocket. I shoved it into the Coke and gave her a five-dollar bill.

When the dancer had finished off the sheriff, and maybe a few of the patrons, I waved at her. She looked at me like, *Oh Jesus what is this* but made her way to my table and sat down.

I took out a business card from Lois Lane's left pocket and said, "Can I ask you a few questions?"

She was younger and prettier than I expected. She had nice hair, a clear complexion and baby blue eyes that were absolutely dead. She gave me a long look before saying, "Not if it's one of those *what's a nice girl like me...*"

"It isn't, I interrupted. "And I assume your first name isn't really *Feather*.

"No. It's Mary."

"Mary Veronica?"

She looked surprised. "How did you know that?"

"Ah…never mind. Were you working last Friday night?"

"Lunch to midnight – the dream shift." Mary Veronica was being ironic, I suspected.

I asked if there was anyone strange in the club that night. She snorted and then laughed out loud. "If anyone ever comes in here that isn't a whack job, you can put that in your paper."

I laughed too, and she started to get up. Suddenly I blurted, "My best friend was murdered." It came out a bit more desperately than I had intended, but she stopped and sat back down.

"You mean the DiSpirito…?" I nodded and there was a fleeting animation in her eyes. "Her sister was a friend of mine in school."

"Really…which one?"

"Tina."

I winced. *Was this kid really that young?*

"Cass was Tina's older sister, and my very good friend."

"I remember her, but what's it got to do with this dive?"

"A Korral Klub matchbook was found at the murder scene." The hell with Speed Bump if he wanted to keep that fact an embarrassing secret, since they'd lost the goddamned thing. He was never going to accomplish anything but forcing people to talk to him who would normally hit him with the nearest blunt instrument. "So it's possible that he was in here some time just before..."

Disgust and a bit of fear crossed her features. "I wouldn't doubt it...I don't remember anyone besides the usual scum balls, but I'll talk to the other girls that were here that night." I took the card and jotted down my home number on the back.

"I hope they find the bastard," she said sincerely.

"*They* may not, but I will. So... am I supposed to pay you for your time or something?"

She looked at me like I was insane and said, "I'll call you if I hear anything. Tell Tina I'm sorry about her sister."

"I will. What's your last name?

"Bartlett. Mary Bartlett." She smiled, as if recalling better times. "She'll remember."

"Thanks for your help. You're a good kid." She rolled her eyes, but I had the feeling that I was right; that she was a good kid.

Escaping from the Klub into the blinding light of day, I walked smack into Walt/Alfred Kobie. He looked at me quizzically and then back at the strippers' photos in the window of the joint from which I had just emerged and said, "Auditioning?" which was pretty funny for him.

"Yes, and they suggested that I stick to singing. What're you doing in this seedy part of the world?"

"The Registry of Motor Vehicles is in this seedy part of the world and I have to renew my license."

"Well, happy birthday."

He looked at me like I couldn't be stupider. "It's not my freakin' birthday," he snapped.

That was the problem with him. Sometimes when you asked the very pleasant Walt a question, the not-so-pleasant Alfred would answer.

He pushed past me, muttering something malevolent and we both went on our way.

**

CHAPTER

North of Boston

The unmarked Crown Victoria started tailing the shiny black Corvette on Route 128 North near the North Shore Shopping Center. To the officer's disappointment, the Vette's operator was not speeding or otherwise law-breaking.

He followed for a mile or so, got bored and slapped the blue bubble light on the car's roof. And for good measure, he hit the siren.

The driver of the Vette, who happened to be Gordon Coelridge Wells the Third, glanced in his rearview mirror and saw Speed Bump gesturing with his fat fist toward the breakdown lane.

"Balls," he muttered, "not *this* fucking idiot."

He steered into the breakdown lane and stopped. As the officer lumbered up to the driver's side door, Gordo stuck his head out of the window and asked in mock fear, "Have I done something wrong, Mr. Policeman?"

"Going kind of fast, weren't you?" Prescott drawled in his best *Smokey and the Bandit* impression.

"If I'd been going fast, you wouldn't have caught me," said the wide-eyed innocent man.

Prescott snorted.

"Yeah, well, follow me back to the station. I have some questions."

Gordon considered leaping of out of the car, grabbing Speed Bump's gun and stuffing it down his throat, which he knew would be no challenge, but a nagging fear suggested that he play along with his friend in blue.

At the station, Speedy led him to a small, stuffy room and told him to wait. An hour passed and Gordo was just about to tell them all to shove it when Prescott returned with a younger officer who was carrying a tape recorder.

The lieutenant took a chair opposite Gordo, leaned back and clasped his hands behind his head. He stared intently at Gordo who stared back.

Finally, Speed broke the silence and asked, "What happened to your girl friend?"

Holding his gaze, Gordo answered slowly.

"I...don't...know. I wish I did." Gordo clenched his fists in his lap.

Prescott righted his chair and leaned toward his suspect, and in a conspiratorial tone said, "She was a handful, wasn't she?"

Gordo suppressed the urge to give Speedy a handful...across his fat face, but forced himself to stay cool.

"She was spirited," he said, smiling sadly.

Speedy nodded in a knowing fashion.

"Now, where were you on Friday night?"

"Here and there," Gordo suddenly felt hot.

"Such as where?" Speed asked, feigning great patience.

"I had a few pops at the Widow," he answered honestly. That was the last thing he remembered.

"What time did you leave there?"

"How should I know?"

"Well, who else would know? Let's cut the crap, Mr. Wells. I believe you met up with Miss DiSpirito, caught her misbehaving and killed her." He chuckled.

"She often misbehaved, didn't she?" Speedy was breathing heavily now and looking more than usual like a gargoyle.

Gordo's face was murderous as he pushed away from the table.

"Go fuck yourself," he suggested, and made for the door. Speedy stood and followed him.

"I'm not finished with this interrogation," he warned.

"Well, I am," Gordo shot back over his shoulder. They both knew Gordo couldn't be held there any longer.

"Don't leave town, Smartass," Speedy shouted after him.

Smartass got into his car and left town.

**

CHAPTER

Port Locke, Massachusetts

The day of Cass's wake was sunny and crisp and altogether wrong. Molly and I attended together since the professor was off on an archaeological dig in El Somewhero. We rode in silence, both wearing sunglasses – Molly because she was intermittently crying and I because of a brutal hangover and the fear that direct sunlight would cause my eyeballs to melt down my face.

We entered Rolimini's Funeral Home from the back door and started toward the front room in the direction that the ghoulish doorman had pointed, looking like the ghost of Christmas Future. It was already mobbed (no pun) with Cass's relatives. I wanted to walk straight through to the front door and out again. I stopped about halfway down the hall, immobilized.

Molly put her hand on my shoulder and pushed me forward. I rounded the doorway on my right. At the other end of the room there was a beautiful white coffin containing the body of Cassandra Yolanda DiSpirito. There were many people ahead of us in the line and when we could finally get to it, Molly and I knelt in front of the casket together. Looking everywhere but at Cass, I silently prayed "Lord, please get me the Christ out of here before I scream."

We blessed ourselves after an appropriate amount of time and when we stood I was face-to-face with Nonnie, who had never shown any affection to anyone that I witnessed. Now she put her claw-like hand on my head and spat out the greeting, *"Youztwo!"* Then she hugged me fiercely and shoved me toward the next grieving relative, Cass's mother. I mumbled inanities at both of Cass's parents and her sister Gina. When I reached Tina, she burst into tears and threw her arms around me. I patted her back and told her that I had a custard in the car. She pulled back and looked at me, puzzled, and I had to consider that Grammy O. was right about Italians not grasping the principles of grief.

Molly gave me an elbow in the ribs and a few minutes later, we were both outside smoking. Yes, Molly smoking. More like just waving it around. A perfect waste of good tobacco.

"Well, that was awful," I observed and was about to congratulate us on how well we had handled things when Molly observed, "I didn't see Gordo."

"It's early. He'll show up." That turned out to be just one of many things that I had wrong that day.

We sat in Molly's VW Bug for a while outside of the funeral home, watching people of whom we disapproved show up.

"Oh sure. There's Chickie DelVecchio coming to mourn her *friend*," I snarled.

Molly offered, "And she's with Lynn Gromano, another of Cassie's dearest pals…"

"Hypocrites," I agreed.

"Jerks."

I expanded upon the theme. "Assholes."

"Why must you swear?"

"The world makes me swear."

"You don't need to swear."

"Oh yes, I do need to swear like a *motherfucker* sometimes, Molly." I shouted.

She looked like I had smacked her in the face. She started the car and squealed out of the parking space. We both sulked all the way to my house and I got out of the car without a word.

I went into the kitchen and spooned the ridiculous custard into the garbage disposal, singing *Bye Bye Custard* to the tune of *Bye Bye Baby* and then suddenly I was bending over the sink, crying and shouting at the gurgling drain, "Damn you, Cassie, you can't be gone."

**

CHAPTER

Bamberg, Germany

Frederich managed the apple cart easily with one hand. It rolled noisily but steadily behind him on its out-of-round wooden wheels. As he reached the crest of the hill and looked down on the marketplace, he was dismayed by the sight of a group of the prince bishop's guardsmen sweeping through the merchants' makeshift aisles and helping themselves to whatever wares they fancied. No one dared to complain.

He groaned inwardly and decided to rest on the hilltop until the guards grew weary of the marauding and went away. He lazed for a while but inactivity was unnatural to him and he eventually rose in disgust and began his descent. Halfway down the incline, he was startled by high-pitched screams coming from the direction of a group of guards that was gathered just beyond the marketplace.

Although he couldn't see what was happening, he recognized the screams as those of a terrified girl or a child. He let go of the cart and began to run toward the fracas and upon reaching the group, parted it by roughly shoving two of the guards out of his way. A girl of about fifteen was lying on the ground with a guard on top of her who was simultaneously attempting to rip off her frock and cover her mouth. Frederich reached down and yanked him up by his neck and punched him squarely in the face. Blood spurted from the soldier's nose.

The group was stunned, but was soon moved to respond. Two of them drew their swords and began to hack at Frederich's back and torso. Not one of them would have dared to take on such a man on their own, but as a pack, their bravado was that of greater men. Frederich fought them all with some success, but when he had finally been overpowered and weakened from injuries; one especially courageous soldier stepped forward and cut his throat. Frederich's last thought was the hope that the girl had managed to escape during the melee.

**

CHAPTER

Port Locke, Massachusetts

Forces unseen had propelled me through Cass's wake, but the funeral was another thing altogether. My parents suggested that I attend with them, but I declined their offer. Despite my tiff with Molly, I asked her to pick me up and we rode to the church in deafening silence.

We pulled up to the curb just past the statue of Our Lady. We had both shuddered as we passed the funeral cars that were parked in a row. Molly shut off the engine and we sat and watched various DiSpirtos, Casabuccis and many of our former Immaculata classmates walk past the car toward the church.

When Molly opened her car door and got out, I found that I couldn't move. She walked around the front of the car and waited on the sidewalk while I continued to sit, staring straight ahead. Finally she opened my door and looked in.

"Come on Kit, we have to do this," she said firmly. My brain sent the message to my legs, but they didn't respond. Molly reached in, grabbed me by the arm and yanked me out of the car.

As we neared the church, three young men in suits were approaching from the other direction, who turned out to be my very own archangel brothers. Without speaking, Doc stepped between Molly and me and took our hands; Michael took Molly's other hand and Raphael took mine. We walked up the church stairs together.

We all genuflected and entered a pew on the left-hand side, about halfway down the aisle. The organist was rendering some depressing piece of noise and Doc and I looked at each other and rolled our eyes. It was the first time I had smiled for days and it lasted for about four seconds.

The church was crowded and there was a murmur and then a hush as Cass's family entered. They passed slowly by our pew -- the women wearing mantilla lace veils and the men in dark suits. My stomach clenched at the sight of Cass's parents and then Nonnie being supported by Angie and one of her sons. Gina and Tina walked behind them, sniffling and holding hands.

The pallbearers consisted of two each Casabucci cousins and DiSpirito cousins and two foremen who worked for DiSpirito Construction. Dave Benjamin, one of the foremen, was madly in love with Cass and didn't care who knew it. His eyes were swollen from crying and a couple of the cousins had to keep flicking tears from their cheeks. Once again, Gordon Wells was not in attendance.

Once the family was seated, the organist ripped into another horrible dirge and the pallbearers began to wheel the casket down the aisle. Hearing the organ made me think of the Heart and Soul incident and I had a terrible urge to laugh. That feeling was short-lived because when the casket reached the first aisle where the family was sitting, Sal DiSpirito began to sob. His huge shoulders shook and he made no effort to contain his grief.

I heard Doc murmur "Poor guy..." as the church began to spin. I reached down and gripped the edge of the pew with both hands, closed my eyes and had my first panic attack. I couldn't catch my breath. I was afraid I was dying and afraid that I wasn't, and would have to put up with feeling this way forever. I could smell the incense and hear people crying but it all seemed far away because of the buzzing in my ears. I was unable to breathe, faint or die.

At communion time, Molly and the archangels had to climb over me to get out of the pew, but I wasn't about to participate in something Cass thought was a straight-up farce. Maybe I'd buy a candy flying saucer if I could find one and give myself communion later. The panic had subsided and I was no longer feeling like I was made of glass that was about to shatter. Now I was stone.

**

CHAPTER

Lake Hamilton, New Hampshire

Gordo had to clean the blood and other fish matter off of the knife before he began to throw it repeatedly at the kitchen wall of his father's pine-paneled fishing cabin.

She was gone.

Bored with the knife-throwing, he let his muscular frame slump onto a kitchen chair. He drained a can of Budweiser and threw it in the sink before reaching into the cooler for another. He had been pounding them down for hours and they hadn't even slightly stilled his pain.

He had loved her and he knew she loved him. How had it gone off the rails like this? For the first time in his life, he was truly sorry for his behavior.

**

CHAPTER

Port Locke, Massachusetts

Every morning after Cass's death, while finding my way back to consciousness, I would slowly become aware that some terrible thing had happened. Then it would hit me physically, like taking a cannonball to the chest. This particular morning, I recalled that I dreamed that Cass and I were sitting on the old grapevine bench and she turned to me and said, "You were right, Kitto. You *are* still inside."

A while later, swallowing hot coffee at my brunch bar, I said aloud, "OK, Cass, what was that supposed to mean?" I had puzzled over it through two more cups when something came back to me. One night when my driver's license was new, my brothers, in a fit of uncharacteristic generosity, let me take their shared hot rod. It was a baby blue '57 Ford Skyliner convertible with a hard top that folded down into the trunk. Cass and I were blasting around the neighborhood in the dark with the top down. Looking up at the treetops, I asked her, "Do you ever feel like you're still *inside* when it's supposed to be *outside*?"

She looked at me for several beats and said "No. No, I don't." She punched the radio on and *Wild Thing* blasted skyward. She started singing lewd alternate lyrics to the song. Such things always amused her and they offended Molly, which amused her even more. Draining my coffee mug, I clearly remembered the way the treetops were illuminated by the streetlights against the dark sky that night; although I hadn't thought of it for years.

Phineas was busy washing his face and gazing at its perfection in the chrome coffee pot when I consulted him. "Could that be what she meant? Blink once for *yes* and twice for *no*."

The cat blinked once, jumped down to the floor and sashayed off.

**

Cass had viewed the advent of shopping malls as the greatest achievement of mankind and our local mall was the center of her universe. In our teen years, the mall had housed some acceptable department stores like Gilchrist's and Jordan Marsh, a few crappy ones like Grant's and just for sheer weirdness, a chapel attached to a store hawking holy Catholic items, all of which was overseen by the order of Carmelite nuns. Whenever we passed that particular display window, Cass would knock on it to get the attention of the tight-faced salesclerks and flip them the bird.

"Not quite ugly enough to be nuns?" she would shout to them. Molly always ran ahead of us when we neared the store.

A week or so after the service for Cass, I was alone in my condo and couldn't find a place to put myself. I sat down at the piano, got up, picked up my electric guitar and put it down again. I knew I had to get out of there. I decided to buy something; preferably something I didn't need. I thought it should be guitar strings which were sold in the record store at the mall of our youth.

I had thought that I might feel better being in a place that Cass had loved, but once I had parked and began walking the storefront sidewalk; memories attacked me from every doorway. When everyone I saw began to look like Cass, I freaked a bit and headed for the Carmelite store/chapel; or the Chapel of Holy Shit, as she had dubbed it.

I entered from the back of the empty chapel and made my way to the section of the altar where, for a price, you were allowed to light a candle and pray. I folded a five-dollar bill and shoved it into the money slot, then lit a candle in the back row of the red glass votive holders.

I sat in the first pew and watched the candle burn. I closed my eyes and said a prayer. I opened my eyes and said another prayer.

A few minutes later, with my heart still hammering, I realized that this exercise was giving me exactly what church rituals had always given me.

Nothing.

**

After my visit to the chapel, I sleepwalked through life, wounded and not knowing what to do about it. My family members were careful not to mention Cass and I didn't know whether I was grateful or irritated.

I stayed numb for a while, thanks to Stolichnaya vodka and ever so healthy thanks to orange juice. In mid-January I took a leave from the paper and also from the OJ, and became a round-the-clock drinker of straight vodka.

I drank in the morning, all afternoon and into the evening. I didn't eat much, and never answered the phone or doorbell. My brother Doc brought me cigarettes, vodka and cat food and lied to the Black Rose about my well-being. Every day, I smoked, drank and listened to music until I attained my goal, which was oblivion. I stopped watching TV when I could no longer see the images on the screen. It went on for weeks.

Early on St. Patrick's Day morning, I awoke gagging on bile. I crawled on my hands and knees to a wastebasket and dry-heaved for what seemed like hours. When it finally ceased, I remained on my knees, wiping tears from my face with the heels of my hands. When finally I raised my eyes to my bedroom ceiling, I whispered three words that I had never strung together before in my life, *"I need help."*

**

I crawled to the phone and called my cousin James who, to the horror of my extended family, had stopped drinking and was living life sober.

He asked me to meet him for coffee (ugh) at four that afternoon. Who drinks coffee at that hour? These sober people must really live an upside-down existence, I thought. Breakfast at night...I'd have to ask him if they ate dinner in the morning.

When Jamie entered the Copper Kettle, he waved and I waved back thinking, *and who the hell is that?* As he approached my booth I recognized him, but his appearance had drastically changed. His coloring was different; he looked healthy and...happy? His face used to be kind of puffy...like mine.

We ordered coffee and talked for hours.

**

My dreams had become a miniseries involving a bunch of people who dressed like Heidi of the Alps and seemed to be trying to tell me a story. They were the most vivid dreams I had ever had and they affected me so much that it sometimes took all day to shake off the emotions that they stirred.

When I awoke with heart palpitations for the third time in one week, I decided to look into the dream thing. I got up, drank three Cokes, opened the Yellow Pages to *Therapists,* closed my eyes and pointed. My random choice turned out to be a Doctor Juliana Starr. I thought it was a good sign that she had the same last name as one of the Beatles.

She answered the phone herself, which threw me a little. "This is Juliana Starr."

"Oh. Uhhhmmmm...I'd like to make an appointment?"

"All right. When would you like to come in?" She had one of those becalmed voices that I find rather irritating.

"Uh, well, sooner is better, I guess…" I tried not to sound too wired, but now that this move had been made, it started to feel kind of urgent.

"I have an opening this afternoon at four," said the Voice of Reason. "Can you make that?"

I agreed and we exchanged some information. I hung up and saw that Phineas was looking at me with his head cocked to the left, indicating interest.

"What?" I asked him. "I'm probably not going. I don't need it. Therapy is for neurotics who can't stop thinking about their own feelings, and I don't need some snot from Radcliffe…" The cat and I stared at each other.

Finally, I said "I know, I know. If you have a toothache, you go to the dentist."

The goddamned cat is always right.

**

At ten of four, I entered the old red brick building where Doctor Starr saw patients – excuse me, *clients*. The anteroom was empty, thank God. I wouldn't want any of my drunken friends or relatives to think I was sick enough to see a shrink. I sat down and opened my battered copy of *The Little Prince*. (I especially liked the story about the planet inhabited by the drinker who only drinks because he's ashamed of his drinking.) Classical music was playing softly and there was a pleasant fragrance wafting from somewhere.

At exactly four o'clock, the door opened and there stood Doctor Starr, the love child of Meryl Streep and Diane Sawyer. Not just attractive, but annoyingly patrician-looking. This would probably not go well, since I immediately doubted her ability to relate to a member of the Harpanwop tribe.

"Gabriella?" she asked quietly. I nodded, closed the book and followed her into the office mumbling, "You can call me Kit."

She told me to sit wherever I'd be comfortable. There was a couch – from which I assumed I was to spill my guts. Fat chance.

The inner walls of the office were red brick and there were pairs of small water color paintings adorning all four walls. I noticed the *J. Starr* signature on one of the two above her desk and asked if she had done them. She nodded.

"They're beautiful," I told her, and they were. I especially liked the one of the Clock Tower Wharf in colonial times. I pointed to a market stall in the painting and said, "This is where I live; just above this crate of chickens. So do I have to lie down?"

"You don't *have to* do anything," she replied serenely.

I wondered briefly if this would end with my bopping her and bolting before my hour was up. I sat on a chair that was directly across from hers, and she and I stared at each other for about five minutes. I don't care for silence unless I have a hangover and since I didn't, I finally said, "My best friend was murdered and I'm having these weird dreams about her and some strange people that I don't know."

She nodded in a noncommittal way and I continued.

"The dreams are recurring, and it seems like every time there's a little more to the story than the time before." I stopped and covered my eyes. "In broad daylight this sounds kind of ridiculous, but when I wake up from these dreams I'm upset beyond reason. I feel like I'm remembering it more than dreaming. I don't know...I...just can't explain it."

I looked at her, and drumming my fingers on the arm of my chair, waited to be cured.

**

I had to admit that I felt better after the session. The good doctor thought that I should come in twice a week, which I saw as overkill, so we agreed on once a week. Therapy might at least stop the dreams. I had mixed feelings about that. They were upsetting, but intriguing. There were no dreams that night but the following night there was a new one.

Just before waking, I dreamed of standing at the rail of the St. John Bridge and looking down at the dark water, wondering if I should jump and thinking that the longer I lived, the more bewildered I became. Cass was dead and that melded into my dream Anke's story where *everyone* was dead and I could muster no hope as I stared down from the bridge.

Suddenly the face of a beautiful blonde child started to float up from the dark water below and rose to where I stood. He looked at me accusingly and I may have shouted out loud. Awake, I was frightened, but more, I was overwhelmed with the certainty that no life, even my own, was mine to take.

**

CHAPTER

Session

At my appointment the next week, I told Doctor S. that during the dreams of Anke's life, I felt responsible for all of the deaths.

"Does that include Cass's death?" she asked.

"Yes," I answered. "No...I don't know. I'm confused about what I feel. I don't even know these people in the dreams, but I feel like I love them."

I chewed my bottom lip and played with the calluses on my fingertips from playing the guitar.

"So you shrinks always answer a question with a question, right?"

Doctor Starr shook her head in the negative and said nothing.

**

CHAPTER

Mannington, Massachusetts

The young woman was, heaven knew, sick to death of men, but this guy looked and acted more human that most of the local talent. They had shared a drink the week before and he had treated her with respect.

She had agreed to go for a sandwich with him when the club closed, and they were on their way to the Night Owl Diner on Route One when he abruptly turned from the turnpike onto an unpaved dark road that ran behind a strip mall of mostly defunct businesses.

Too late she realized that they weren't going to the diner and too late she saw the knife.

**

The next morning, it was Sam Zaticone, the driver of a disposal service truck that found the body of Mary Veronica Bartlett behind a non-operational beauty supply store. He spotted her blonde hair in his side mirror as the truck raised the dumpster and jumped down from the truck's cab hoping to help her, but it was obvious from a closer look at her face that there was nothing to be done except to call the police.

Sam was a gentle family man and was sickened by his gruesome discovery. He quit his job that day and opened a successful no-kill animal shelter.

**

CHAPTER

Port Locke, Massachusetts

"Jesus Christ, Molly, tell me I didn't get that kid killed," I barked into the phone just as it was picked up.

"What are you talking about?"

"The body that was found today was the dancer that I talked to at the Korral Klub the other day."

"You mean that friend of Tina's?"

"Yes, dammit! Who the hell is doing these things?" I wailed. "She didn't know anything about this crap."

"Well," Molly said. "Someone must have thought she did. Are you all right?"

"Hell, no."

**

CHAPTER

Session

The first stupid question I asked the doctor in my next session while looking out of her office window was, "Are the buds on the trees always this green?"

She eyed me warily and said, "Why do you ask?"

I gave her my "thought you didn't always answer a question with a question" look and said, "I don't know. They just look different."

"Maybe you're just seeing them differently."

"That's possible. I guess I've spent a lot years not looking up." This sounded strangely tragic, once uttered.

"How long have you been sober now?" she asked.

"I don't know exactly. Somewhere around three months, one week, two days (I looked at my watch) seven hours and twenty-eight minutes."

"Good."

"Oh it's good, all right. It's so good I could go into primal screams."

"Go ahead," she said, smiling.

She could be really annoying.

Having gotten off to this weird start, I decided to plunge right in and bluntly stated, "I think that in the dreams, I'm Magda."

She did her barely perceptible nod.

"It's like …I lived her life."

She stared.

"How can it be so real? Most dreams are just a bunch of screwball stuff that doesn't make any sense. These aren't like that…"

I felt ridiculous verbalizing these things, but I soldiered on. "I feel like I know these people and really care about them. And I don't even know who they are."

"Are you sure?" she asked quietly.

I was startled out of my conversation with myself.

"Sure of what? That I don't know who they are?" I asked, and she nodded in the affirmative.

"Yes, I'm sure! They're like characters in a movie or something. They live in the forest primeval and dress like they're going to a Halloween party. How could I possibly know them?"

She shrugged and stared.

"I feel like they're trying to tell me…something important."

We were silent for a few minutes.

"The moral of which…" I gestured to my right temple and continued, "is *in here* and I can't get it. I had a crazy dream about Cass, too, where she handed me this huge cake. There were candles burning all around the edges, and she pointed to some lettering in the center that said WHAT YOU DON'T KNOW. The letters started melting and when I looked for Cass, she was gone."

We were both silent for a while when she suddenly asked if I had been a blackout drinker.

"No," I indignantly assured her.

"How would you know?"

Now I stared.

She was really, really annoying, but she had a point. How *did* people know if they had blackouts, since by definition they wouldn't know?

**

CHAPTER

Port Locke, Massachusetts

Molly sat across from me in a booth at the Copper Kettle where I was indulging my new addiction – coffee, which can make you more nuts than alcohol.

After I elaborated on my reaction to the news of Mary Bartlett's death, Molly remarked, "This isn't funny, Kit."

"No shit. Am I laughing?"

She glared at me for swearing, but I felt like punishing her for her past unkind sentiments toward our late lamented friend. She sensed it and said, "I lost Cass, too, you know."

"I know that," I snapped. She was right.

"Kit, you're in danger if you led someone to kill that girl."

"Gee, thanks."

"Then they're after you, too."

"Thanks again."

"You should come and stay with me and Sacha."

"Sacha? Did you get a cat?"

"David has forsaken Western philosophy and changed his name."

"What a blow for Western philosophy. Do they know?"

She ignored that and went on, "We have an extra room. He's got a Buddhist altar set up in there but…"

"No thank you. I can't go and hide. Where would that end?"

"Seriously, you shouldn't be alone and with us, you'd be protected."

"For how long? Believe me, if someone decides to kill you, there isn't a goddamned thing you can do about it."

"That's a great attitude, and don't swear."

"It's the truth," I replied.

"Why don't you stay at your parents?"

"Because then I'd be looking for someone to kill me."

Exasperated, she demanded, "Will you at least not run around in sleazy dangerous places playing detective?"

"Well, someone has to. Have these murders been solved and no one told me? Do you really think the idiots on our police force can handle it? Half of them can't write their own names, and I know this well from reading their attempts at handwriting on my numerous tickets."

"Please just promise to be careful."

"Yes, Mother. May I go now?"

She shook her head in disgust and I slid out of the booth.

**

I left the Copper Kettle and at the Oracle Book Store, I paused to look at a slim volume that was prominently featured in the window, about Edgar Cayce, the Sleeping Prophet. I had heard of him and presumed that the sleeping prophet thing was an act, but I decided for no clear reason to go in and buy the book. I had been reading more now that I wasn't cross-eyed from alcohol.

The store smelled of sandalwood incense, which I rather liked, so I bought three packages of the sticks and a burner shaped like a wizard's head that featured holes in his hat for the escaping smoke. I wanted to ask if they had one where the smoke came out of his ass but the clerk who rang up the sale was a rather severe-looking woman with no-color short hair and glasses, and I suspected that she wouldn't enjoy the joke. Cass would probably have asked her what she charged to haunt the place.

I spent the rest of the day reading the Cayce book. It was disturbingly believable. He had found all manner of cures for people who had strange physical maladies and uncovered the root causes of psychological problems for others, often connecting them to a past-life experience.

The Cayce material piqued my interest in reincarnation and I returned to The Oracle Book Store where I bought another dozen books relating to the topic. I devoured them and went back for more. I was especially fascinated with stories about people being hypnotized and regressed. There were documented cases of people speaking in languages they didn't know and describing places that they had never seen.

I was intrigued with the eternity of soul concept and earning your way into paradise at your own speed. It made so much more sense than the absurd mortal sin system that I had learned whereby missing mass was accorded the same status as mass murder. We had been fed nonsense that no thinking person should have swallowed.

To wit, when we were children, in order to be worthy of the communion host, we were required to fast from midnight on Saturday night to whatever point in time we attended Mass the next day. People fainted, people vomited; diabetics went into shock and died.

My mother once shared a story wherein a girl ate a piece of candy before going to mass and decided to receive communion anyway. When she attempted to rise, she found that she was nailed to the pew. I was seven and my brother

Doc was nine and we were aghast at first, but the more we thought about it, the sillier the story became.

Doc looked the Black Rose directly in the eye and said, "You believe that?"

When my father chuckled from the other room, the Black Rose frowned and said, "Of course I believe it. Nuns don't lie."

**

I became a regular at the Oracle, where I had seen postings for psychics who did past-life regressions, and decided to look into doing one. The same stern-faced clerk was working and she turned out to be quite accommodating. In response to my questions, she took a business card from under the counter and told me, "This is the best route for getting in touch with your former selves." She then crossed out the store's contact information and penciled in *Ling Lee 781 555 0531.*

I had a lot of time to fill up now that I didn't drink. I was pretty much on my own since my family was taboo, Cass was gone and Molly and Doyle were shocked and dismayed by my sobriety.

I went home and called Ling Lee for an appointment.

**

Ling Lee was old and stooped and the yellowed skin that stretched over his facial bones looked like faded paper money.

"Mr. Lee?" *Was it Mr. Lee or Mr. Ling? I'm..."*

"You come," he said, then turned around and padded softly down the hall in what appeared to be little black slippers. Ling/Lee was a man of few words.

He stopped at a doorway on the right side of the hall and entered. I followed him into a darkened room where a fountain trickled in one corner and incense burned in another. Soothing music tumbled from a speaker in the ceiling. It was a bit reminiscent of my first visit to Doctor Starr's office. That had turned out all right, I assured myself, even though I was sure that comparing Ling Lee to Doctor Starr was like comparing P. T. Barnum to Carl Jung.

He motioned toward what looked like a dentist's chair in the middle of the room and I sat down on it stiffly. He walked over, leaned down and flipped a lever on the side of the chair that caused the back to lower so that I was in an almost prone position.

And what have you set yourself up for this time? asked my bothersome conscience. As I was constructing an acceptable answer, Mr. Ling/Lee leaned over and smeared some kind of oil on the middle of my forehead.

"Okay, okay. Terd eye," he sing-songed.

Had he just called me Turd Eye? He walked around the chair several times then stopped behind my head. I felt something touch my forehead in the spot where he had put the oil, but it didn't hurt.

"To close eyes," said he, which I was none too anxious to do, but since I'd asked for all this, I did it.

Instantly, I saw several women gathered at the edge of a body of water. As I approached the group, the sound of the water cascading over rocks grew louder. The women were dressed in loose-fitting gowns. They appeared to be filling up stone containers with water, laughing and talking as they worked.

Suddenly, there was shouting from the other side of the river and the women stopped what they were doing, shaded their eyes with their hands, and looked across the water anxiously.

A group of soldiers on horseback came into view, and stopped at the water's edge. The women dropped the water vessels and began to run toward me. One of them slipped her arm through mine urging, "Run, Layla, run!"

My heart had started to pound when, as suddenly as if I had changed a television station, I was looking at a ship in the distance. I felt a rocking sensation and realized that I was on a boat, holding onto a brass deck rail. I heard someone high above me shout, "Spanish! She's Spanish!" Again I felt the heart-stopping fear and the image dissolved into another.

Anke's face, which I had seen in the dreams, was suddenly before me, bathed in perspiration. She was advising me not to look so stricken, that she was only giving birth, with which I seemed to be reluctantly assisting. As her face contorted and she opened her mouth to scream out her joy at the miracle of birth, another image appeared.

I was in a church singing in the sweetest sounding choir I've ever heard. The words weren't English, but I understood them at the time. There was a similar vision where I was playing a huge pipe organ in a beautiful cathedral and singing in yet another language.

I began to relax into the rhythm of the images and realized that when what I viewed became frightening, something less threatening instantly replaced it.

I'm not able to recall all of the images, but I gradually knew with absolute certainty that there was a reason and a perfect order to what I was being shown. Near the end, the pictures changed rapidly, as if someone was sitting on a remote control, but I was awash in perfect calm. I remember laughing at myself for dismissing a divine plan when I rejected Catholicism. I had thrown the baby out with the bathwater because it had been beyond me to comprehend that it wasn't God that was a train wreck, it was religions, and they were train wrecks that were mostly caused by people bringing their own self-serving baggage aboard.

From this torrent of people and places, I sensed and understood that there was a karmic law, and with a sublime clarity that no drug could have produced, I understood that it was a system of perfect justice, and it filled me with a boundless joy.

**

That feeling lasted for a few days. However, in addition to my new state of sobriety making me hyperconscious (I could feel and hear my skin cells regenerating) as my alcoholic numbness disappeared, I began to remember more clearly the exploits of the past and to seriously question if we had been half as entertaining as we thought we were. At the end I was unable to function like a human. I couldn't work, think straight or get through one day not drinking. The *who-gives-a-shit* attitude was gone and I was becoming mildly embarrassed by certain memories. It wasn't pretty.

I decided to walk over to Nelly's and buy a half gallon of their no-name chocolate ice cream for which I had developed more than a taste. I added two packages of Vantage cigarettes to that order and left happily enough, anticipating my upcoming binge of chocolate and nicotine. That may be why I was blindsided by what happened next.

Walking down the wharf, I gathered Lois Lane's collar around my neck as the wind whipping up from the water found its way directly into my bones. I tried not to, but I made the mistake of glancing over at the Frig. The buggy had been removed by the police, and its absence chilled me as much as its presence would have.

Although the worst horror of my life had occurred there, contrasted with the gloomy dusk, the bar's indoor lights glowed warmly and the flashing neon HEINEKEN BEER sign seemed to be beckoning to me personally. I wanted nothing more than to walk over to that door. But I didn't. Once inside my condo, I was safe and sober, but knew for certain that I would never be warm again.

**

CHAPTER

Session

At my therapy appointments, I spent a lot of my money enlightening Doctor Starr on a number of subjects. One morning I was holding forth on the effectiveness of alternate belief systems.

"What's the difference between a spell and a prayer?" I railed at her. "I know you'll just tell me that I want to think I have some mysterious power because I'm socially impotent or…"

She looked genuinely surprised and interrupted me (a first).

"*Socially impotent*? Are you serious?" she asked incredulously.

"Well, yuh. Why?"

"You're smart, you're funny…I actually look forward to our sessions."

"And yet you charge me." I observed.

She laughed and said, "See what I mean?"

"No, I don't," I answered truthfully.

I stared at her and waited for her to elaborate. She didn't, but she started to smirk (another first). I waited some more.

She shook her head slowly and said, "*So* frustrating."

"Ha!" I said. "I knew I could break you. I warned you that I was much more likely to make you crazy than you were to make me sane."

"We're both sane and thankfully our time is up," she deadpanned.

I rose from the couch (I continued to resist lying down) and turned around to search behind. "You know, I had a friend who was whining to her shrink that no one ever listened to her and just as she said it, she caught him looking above her head at the clock behind her."

She sighed wearily and said, "Please get out."

"See you next week," I said and went out the exit door. Shrinks always have two doors to prevent their clientele from spotting each other and assuming that the other one's nuts.

**

CHAPTER

Port Locke, Massachusetts

Following the Ling/Lee visit, I had hurried home to make notes about my visions in my official investigative reporter notebook. For the rest of that day and night, I felt a sense of peace and safety. I went to bed and had no disturbing dreams.

The next morning I fired up a pot of coffee and *Highway 61 Revisited* for inspiration. (Why does the guitar on *Queen Jane Approximately* sound out of tune to me? Surely Mike Bloomfield would have noticed.) With the help of Mr. Dylan and Mrs. Folger, I reviewed my notes and began to see a pattern emerging. I drew diagrams with arrows, erased them and chewed the pen. I got up and paced. I shared the work with Phineas.

"Could this be? Is this the *Universal Truth?*" I demanded, shoving the diagram in front of his furry face as he stretched out his front legs unapologetically in a basket of clean laundry. He glanced at the diagram, yawned, blew his Friskies-fouled breath at me and collapsed into nap mode.

By noontime I was speeding on caffeine and high on my splendid discoveries. I called Molly at her father's bar. Her master's degree in Anthropology had been a great help with her lunch gig there. Speaking at five hundred words a minute, I said,

"I've gotta talk to you. It's really, *really* important. Can you come over here right away? I mean like now?"

"What?" She could barely hear me over the noise in the bar. Her father's lunch clientele weren't exactly executives.

"We've got to talk!" I hollered into the phone.

Marjorie Campbell

"About what?" she hollered back.

"The meaning of life," I yelled.

"No, really…"

(Deliver me.)

"Just come over here after work, all right?"

"All right, all right…I'll be over." She hung up.

**

I buzzed Molly in about three o'clock and before she had her coat off or was able to finish the sentence that began, "Those creeps at the Drum are so cheap…" I had thrust my untidy diagram in her face.

"Look at this, look at this," anxious for her to share my joy.

"Fine, thanks and you?" she sniffed. Taking the notebook from me, she sat down on a stool at the brunch bar and looked at the scrawled mess before her.

"OK, I give up, and I've had cryptology courses. What is this?"

I grabbed the notebook back and said, "Look, see these arrows? This is who we were and this is who we are now."

She looked blank for a moment and shook her head. "Kit, you really need to start drinking again…"

"No, I don't. Listen. It's all right here and it *works*. Look at the diagram. Anke was Cass, I was Magda and you were the little boy, Emil."

"Thanks. I appreciate your making me the little boy."

"I didn't make you the little boy, you did. You chose your new incarnation between lifetimes."

She rolled her eyes. "Of course I did."

"I know it sounds out there, but how else can you explain all this?" I asked.

"All *what*?" I wasn't getting through.

I motioned a circle and said, "This, all of it...the world." Pointing at the names on the diagram, I said "Us, them, everyone..."

She leaned back against the brunch bar, looking confused. "Seriously, what are you talking about?"

"Reincarnation, that's it...that's the answer..."

"To what question?

"*The* question, the big one," I shouted.

She slid off of the stool and said, "Oh, that one." She picked up her coat.

"I sense a lack of interest. Did you not seek higher learning while Cass and I sought just to *be* higher? Are you not a scholar?"

"Oh, yes...that's why they gave me this nice scholar uniform." She ran her hands down the lapels of her black bartender vest and said brightly, "Hey, why don't we go on another island vacation? Maybe Dottie would stand in for Cass."

"No one stands in for Cass, Molly. *No one*."

"All right, all right. By all means, continue with your diatribe."

"You know I was having those dreams, and I just had an acupuncture third-eye reading done and I know for sure that those people in the dreams were real and they were *us*."

She shook her head, narrowed her eyes and said, "You just had a *what?*"

"I had this Chinese guy stick a needle in my third eye..."

She slumped back down on the stool, raised her eyebrows and said, "Third eye? You have a third eye that I never noticed?"

I tapped impatiently on the middle of my forehead. "Right here, everyone's got an invisible third eye..."

"Well, I'm glad they're invisible."

I scowled at her and pressed on.

"Anyway...I saw visions of past lives, of all of us being together in the past, over and over...you, Cass, our families ... the same souls living lives together and coming back to work out their karma..."

She slapped herself in the head and held up her hand like a traffic cop. "Stop. You dragged me over here just to listen to one of your anti-Catholic rants?"

I paused mid-rant and generously explained, "You really must divest yourself of the guilt that the nasty nuns heaped upon you for your alleged naughtiness."

Molly still attended Mass, even though she no longer believed in God. Cass and I thought that she was still atoning for the *Holy God/Heart and Soul* incident.

"*Catholics!*" I continued, and made a spitting gesture. "They've never gotten anything right. They fear women, they hate children and by the way, Western religions are the only ones that *don't* embrace reincarnation."

"Now you sound like Dav...Sacha," she observed.

"That was uncalled for," I huffed, but continued. "And, for your continuing education, a huge portion of the world believes this, so it isn't something that I just dreamed up in my sleep."

"Yes, it kind of was…"

"Well, okay…but come on, you can't be so narrow-minded that you're not willing to even consider this."

She sighed and looked out the window. "Have you got any beer?"

"I have some alcohol-free beer."

"Why would I want fake beer?"

"You don't. I do. I keep it around in case of crisis."

"Why would you want fake beer in a crisis?"

"I don't know!" I snapped. "Maybe it's a fake crisis."

"It'd better be," she observed dryly.

"I might have some vanilla," I sneered and then relented. "I think Doc left a half a bottle of Stoli under here."

Think? I knew. In fact, I could have drawn a picture of exactly how full it was. (This was just another nod toward being prepared for crisis, like snakebite.) I withdrew the bottle from the nearly empty cabinet below the kitchen counter that had once been home to my impressive inventory of alcohol.

I wasn't thrilled that she could drink the vodka and that I couldn't; I mean, didn't want to. I pushed the bottle across the counter to her and asked unkindly, "Will a glass be needed or do you want to inject it directly into your liver?"

"A glass would be nice," she said quietly. A brief, regretful look passed between us because we both knew that a shared passion that we had for so long was no more.

"Now just humor me for a minute and listen," I instructed once she had twisted up a Cape Codder and sipped. Molly could make a cocktail faster than any living human and fry six hamburgers at the same time.

I leaned the notebook up against the bottle of Stoli for balance...or maybe to block the bottle from view.

"Haven't you ever met someone you instantly liked or disliked?

She thought for a moment and said, "Yes, *you*. I instantly disliked you because you had a big family."

"Pfffftt...lucky me. Seriously, haven't you ever felt like you've always known someone, even though you haven't?"

"No...I don't know...maybe."

"So maybe Cass was Anke," I suggested.

"And I was a little *boy*." She was still finding that idea unacceptable.

"Yes, you were her son."

"Then you'd think we'd have gotten along better," she said, shrugging.

"Not necessarily. This could be why you two were always at odds. The kid thought she had abandoned him."

"Did she?"

"Yes, but she didn't want to. She was charged with witchcraft and executed. And she did give him to someone who would protect him; who did a spectacularly bad job."

"So she gave me, I mean *him*, to you?"

"Me and my brother, who may have been his father," I said.

"May have been? Well, that part sounds like Cass."

We both laughed and then she asked, "So, was she a witch?"

"No. Yes. Well, sort of. She was a wise woman; a healer who had Second Sight, like ESP or psychic power. The Church believed that a woman should have no demonstrable power…"

She sighed and said, "I know, I know. Mother Church is at the root of all evil…"

"Not all of it, just a hell of a lot," I countered. "And this is not my opinion; this is fact. In Europe, they burned tens of thousands of "witches" and anyone who didn't like it."

"Tens of *thousands*?" she asked skeptically.

"Yes, some estimates are higher; maybe millions."

She looked away, then back, and asked, "And for what reason would they do such a thing?"

"To convert the world. Do you know that every Christian holiday miraculously falls on or near a pagan holiday? They were trying to wipe out goddess-based religion and since the population was accustomed to celebrations at certain points in the year, the church gave them some, by inventing matching feasts and celebrations."

I said all of that in one breath.

"Don't have any more coffee, OK?" Moll suggested. I was a bit torqued.

"All right, but let me give you an example. One of the Old Religion celebrations was the feast of the goddess Esther. It was celebrated in the spring and associated with eggs, baskets and bunny rabbits. Sound familiar? Christianity's *Easter* coincidentally shows up."

Molly smirked in disbelief, but I continued.

"The goddess-based religions celebrated the feast of Esther on the first Sunday after the first full moon after the vernal equinox. The Catholic church still determines the date of Easter Sunday by that formula."

"You're nuts!"

"Ask a priest if you don't believe me. And the birth date of Jesus? It was simply lined up with the celebration of the Winter Solstice. The nativity story doesn't match the facts in terms of the seasons, stars, and a few other little details."

Molly held her palms to her forehead. "Where are you getting this stuff?" She picked up her glass and drained it.

**

"Well Kit, thanks for explaining the universe." Molly said to me over her shoulder as I followed her to the front door. Having drained the vodka bottle, she was a bit wobbly and, I thought, somewhat sarcastic. When she opened the front door, a light-colored flash flew past us and out into the darkness.

It would seem that one of the truly fun parts of being a cat is that you can make no move toward a door during a thousand openings and then surprise your human pals by making a break for it once they've been lulled into believing that you've no interest in the outside world.

Panicked, we both ran into the dark parking lot. Molly quickly produced a flashlight from her glove compartment and we spent the next twenty minutes making kitty noises while I repeated *shit, shit, shit* and she prayed to Saint

Anthony. There was no moon and the parking lot lighting was more inadequate than usual. We ducked and looked under the cars where we probably couldn't have seen him anyway.

"Phinney!" I shouted, nearing hysteria, and the lights went on in the condo unit of the Twinnie Winnies. Two tiny heads appeared at their front window. Just as I was about to flip them off, Molly shook my shoulder yelling, "Look!" and pointed to my living room window.

Phineas was lying on top of the couch-back, gazing out of the bay window at us. His tail swished back and forth laconically and his eyes were half closed. Apparently he had changed his plans while we were searching like idiots beneath vehicles and now he was worn out from watching us.

Molly lowered herself into the seat of her VW snarling, "Do you wonder why I'm a dog person?"

My body nearly disintegrated in relief. "Thank God he's all right. Nighty night, Molly."

"Please call me Emil," she said, making a cuckoo motion beside her head while she revved the engine. She backed out and sped off.

"She's so funny," I mumbled, hurrying back to the open door before the cat decided to embark upon another adventure.

**

CHAPTER

Port Locke, Massachusetts

Against my better judgment and the rare spoken-out-loud advice of Doctor Starr, I attended my family's Christmas Eve Drink-a-thon. This year it was held at the home of my cousin Kevin – brother of my sober cousin Jamie, who had the good sense to stay away.

Their father, my uncle Terrence, was married to my mother's sister Teresa (they were Aunt Terry and Uncle Terry, which could only happen in my family) and on this Yule eve, he appeared to have oversampled his famous mega-proof eggnog.

He had chosen me to harangue about the state of Massachusetts and their *goddam welfare* program, which he apparently thought I had some hand in creating. He accentuated his points with karate chops to the kitchen stove. I could have pointed out that he lived in New Hampshire and it wasn't exactly his tax money he was talking about, but I knew that disagreeing with a drunk was a losing proposition. First, it's what they want and second, you're trying to reason with a mental case.

Finally I held up a finger (not the one I would have preferred) and quickly made my way to the bathroom. I hid there for a little while then sneaked into a bedroom where my coat had been flung on the bed with about sixty-five others, grabbed it and left without a fa-la-la-la-la to anyone.

Back at t home, I drank cider and smoked cigarettes. I tried to watch the Lockhart version of *A Christmas Carol*, but I found myself wanting to see Scrooge kick Tiny Tim's crutch out from under him.

Reflecting on my escape from Uncle Terry, I recalled seeing people staring at me and then excusing themselves during some of my better discourses. When had that started? Maybe I hadn't been holding my firewater any better than those infuriating relatives that I had sworn that I would never become. It was a not so merry Christmas thought.

**

CHAPTER

Session

"Maybe having my head smashed in opened up an area of my brain that's tapping into these memories."

Doctor S. nodded, "Possibly. There have been near death experiences recorded that appear to have caused that kind of thing."

She turned around, took a slim volume from her bookcase and handed me *Journeys to Joy* by Desmond Kincaid. "These are records of NDE's. Why don't you read it?"

"But I didn't have an NDE. My heart never stopped. And there were no angels playing harps or anything. It was more like I was just resting, in between running into dead celebrities. Anyway, here's the thing."

I took my diagram from my pocket and began, "I think that I was Magda, Cass was Anke and Molly was Emil. Maybe Gordo was Frederich. Maybe the bastard who killed Cass was the guard who tortured her, or the bishop. They were both assholes."

I looked up at her to see if she was rolling on the floor laughing yet, but she gave me her usual non-committal look.

I laughed, "I know, I know -- and my mailman was Katherine of Aragon. But no one is claiming to be Cleopatra here. These are all just ordinary people."

I read her book that night. There were cases where people who could barely add two and two got struck by lightning and woke up with the ability to do advanced calculus. What struck me was that when people experience death and return to their bodies, they're not all that happy about it. No one comes back and says, *Hey, it's great to be back here in Fresno.*

**

CHAPTER

Port Locke, Massachusetts

I woke up at four in the morning, knowing that something was wrong. Thanks to Uncle Slug, I have a heavy police-issued flashlight that I keep beside my bed for the purpose of injuring and subduing intruders. I picked it up and turned on my bedside lamp. It was almost dawn.

I started for the living room calling to Phineas, praying that an opportunity for escape hadn't been created by my nocturnal visitor.

"Phinney?" I called as I crept down the hallway. I hoped it sounded like I was calling to some brute that would assist in the killing of the unwelcome guest. The cat was nowhere in sight and the front door was open a foot or so.

"Phinney!" I shouted again. *"Oh nononononononono…"*

I ran out of the front door in my jammies and looked around. The brick steps were cold and I scurried back in for shoes. Passing the bathroom, I stopped, stepped in and with the flashlight held aloft like a club, yanked back the shower curtain. Phineas was asleep on a towel that he had pushed into the tub for his rest and comfort.

Relieved but exasperated, I shouted, "A braver beast might have warned me of the intruder…and a dog would have eaten him." I thought that last part would really get to him but he just yawned and looked like I was boring him to death and had a hell of nerve waking him up.

I went back to the living area and noticed that the Bob head collection was askew. Cass, Molly and I were smiling happily in the three pictures that were hung on the wall above the Bob heads. My guest had smashed the glass of all three frames precisely at my face.

**

I called the police and two officers showed up. Mercifully, neither of them was Speed Bump. One was Arthur "Mack" Macklin, who was a friend of the archangels and the other an older woman officer, who looked at me sympathetically and said, "Scary, huh?"

I showed them the picture frames and Mack examined the door jamb. There was no damage.

"Who has a key?" he asked.

"Just me and my brother Doc. Oh, and Cass had one."

"Maybe you should check with her family to see what happened to it."

"Okay," I said, knowing I would do no such thing. The DiSpiritos and I were now only painful reminders of terrible grief to each other. I had demonstrated that to myself the day I spotted Gina at the mall and turned around and left. I had the feeling she'd have done the same.

"I might have left it unlocked. I really can't remember," I said. The law took their leave and I cleaned up the mess and called Molly.

**

The next day, I had a call from Jakey Stonecroft, the delightfully insane owner of *The Friar in the Well*, a coffeehouse in Port Locke named for an old Celtic folk song. Grammy O. knew the song but would never sing it because she said it was dirty and only an English Protestant could have written it.

I generally didn't enjoy playing there because their idea of a drink was pomegranate juice with a lime rind. But now that I was sober, I thought it might be fun to dust off some of the old folk songs that I'd learned in my teens and not have people slobbering boozy requests at me or asking to hear the same song seventeen times in a row.

Cass had been fascinated by the song behind the coffeehouse's name and had insisted that we learn it. We harmonized to it when in our cups; in other words, frequently. Because the name was so weird, Jakey was frequently asked to explain it. He decided to hand-print the dirty Protestant verses to the song in medieval calligraphy on the back of each menu and people were referred thereto when curious. This is the story:

THE FRIAR IN THE WELL

It's of an old friar as I have been told,
(Fal-the-dal-diddle-i-dee)
He courted a young maid just sixteen years old,
(Fal-the-dal-diddle-i-dee)
He came to the maid as she lay on her bed,
And swore he would have her maidenhead,
To my fero-lero-liddle,
Sing twice to my lanky-down-derry-O!

"Oh, no!" said the maid, "For you know very well
If we do such things we should go to Hell."
"No matter, my dear, you need have no doubt
If you were in Hell I could sing you out."

"Oh, then", said the maid, "you shall have this thing
But you to me ten shillings must bring."

And while he went home the money to fetch
She thought to herself how the old friar she could catch.

Now while he was gone, the truth to tell
She hung a cloth in front of the well,
He knocked at the door, the maid let him in,
"Oh now, my dear, Oh let us begin."

Then "Alas!" cried the maid, all crafty and cunning,
"I think I hear my father a-coming."
So behind the cloth the old friar did trip
And into the well he happened to slip.

The friar called out with a pitiful sound,
"Oh, help me out or I shall be drowned."
"You said you could sing my soul out of Hell
Well, now you can sing yourself out of the well."

So she helped him out and bid him be gone
And the friar he wanted his money again,
"Oh, no" said the maid, "I'll have none of the matter
For indeed you must pay me for dirtying the water."

So out of the house the old friar did creep
Dripping his arse like a newly-dipped sheep
And young and old commended the maid
For the very pretty trick that she had played.

Toting my acoustic guitar on my back like a good folkie, I entered the Friar and walked smack into Jakey, who threw his arms around me and kissed my cheek.

"Poor Cassie...I can't believe it." He shook his head and patted my shoulder. "Remember when she wanted me to paint her a picture of the friar splashing around in the well?"

We both laughed and I said, "She got a real bang out of *ye olde friar,* all right. But I think she wanted a picture of him actually drowning in the well."

"That she did," Jakey agreed, smiling and stroking his sandy beard. He was an artist who will probably be famous in a hundred years. For now, he ran the coffeehouse that barely paid for itself and a small gallery that did pretty well during the summer. His oils, particularly the seascapes, were masterful and tourists loved them.

Molly brought the professor (Sacha/David) to this gig. He actually liked the pomegranate juice and probably liked that Moll couldn't drink there.

While singing the twenty-two verses to *Matty Groves,* I was recalling when we had first met Molly's boyfriend, David Armand Gage. He was a professor of things anthropologic at the College of New England and was eighteen years her senior. Cassie was turned off by his age, his skinny physique (she liked them rugged) and his balding head.

"Is that allowed?" Cass had asked Molly. "He's a teacher and you're a student."

"I'm not a student. I'm teaching on a fellowship. And we're all adults."

Like my brother Doc, Molly was a career coed, and looking down her academic nose at Cass was one of her favorite pastimes. Cass was bright; she just saw little point in the quest for knowledge. She found the quest for accessories much more meaningful.

"Isn't it kind of like dating your father?" Cass pressed.

"I don't know. I never dated my father," Molly snarled.

"Play nice, kiddies, play nice," I warned, thinking *all adults, my arse.*

**

After my set, I joined Molly and Sacha/David, who was looking around approvingly at the medieval setting. The doors were short and rounded at the top and the hardware was made of a black hammered metal. Candles burned in lanterns on each of the wooden wine casks that served as tables. Jakey had sketched a number of whimsical knight-themed charcoals that hung at irregular positions on the walls. The fireplace blazed, completing the cozy, rustic feel of the place on this winter night.

"How did you get this job?" the professor asked.

"Judy Collins must have called in sick. You should try their sawdust muffins. They're delightful."

"Please, I work up enough of a thirst in here," Molly observed.

That remark prompted me to say "Well, if Cass had worried less about her thirst, she might still be here."

Molly looked surprised and raising her voice said, "So people who drink deserve to be killed?"

"That is NOT what I said, Molly," I hollered back.

The Friar is a mellow place and people began to look in our direction disapprovingly for messing with their serenity.

Molly flapped her hands up and down in a *quiet down* gesture. "So we should all stay home and watch television?" she hissed. She thought that people who watched television were morons. To this day, she couldn't name two characters on the *Mary Tyler Moore Show*. It's just un-American.

"Well, if Cass had been watching television..." I shook my head. "Never mind, I don't know where that came from."

"I do," Molly said cryptically.

I looked at her questioningly but she didn't elaborate. I said, "It's just that I miss her so much."

"I know, Kit, me too," Molly replied, touching my elbow.

The professor nodded his head like he understood and I think that he did.

**

CHAPTER

Session

"Maybe it's just that it's so deliciously un-Catholic, but the reincarnation thing really makes sense to me," I said.

The doctor stared.

"I mean, at least it's a system of justice – which is far more than my former religion ever offered."

More staring.

"Are you writing a grocery list in your head?" I asked.

She looked puzzled and then laughed.

"I'm listening."

"What did I just say?"

"That you're finding the reincarnation theory more believable than what Catholic doctrine teaches."

"Do you believe in reincarnation?" I asked.

She shook her head. "That doesn't matter."

"It does to me."

"It shouldn't. We're here to talk about you."

"Do you think you look like Meryl Streep?" I asked.

"A little," she replied.

"Okay, now that we're talking about you, do you believe in reincarnation?"

She covered her eyes with her hands and shook her head. I can be annoying, too.

**

CHAPTER

Bamberg, Germany

The knock on the door was soft, but Magda was alarmed. Farmers had little time for socializing and a visit often meant that a disaster had occurred. She opened the door and two workers from the neighboring farm stood with their hats in their hands, their expressions somber. Her heartbeat quickened.

"Emil?" she asked breathlessly, and the two men shook their heads and said, "No." Magda's eyes moved to the cart behind them. It was Frederich's apple cart. She briefly froze at the sight of the tip of Frederich's boot protruding from under the animal skin covering that he often used to protect the fruit.

Magda rushed past her visitors to the cart and tore the covering from her brother's bloodied body. She gasped, then turned slowly to the older of the two farm hands and said, "Please go around back and get Emil. Take him away until I come for him."

The man nodded and turned to go. Heinrich, the younger man, who had been a childhood friend to Frederich, came to her side and said, "I'll help."

They carried the body into the cottage. Magda drew water from the well and together they undressed and bathed Frederich, then dressed him in clean clothes. Magda was stoic throughout the ritual while Heinrich explained what had happened; that her brother had been killed by the bishop's sadistic bullies, while defending a helpless girl. When she thanked him for his help, he hugged her awkwardly, shrugged his shoulders and left. Magda closed the door behind him and fell to the floor, weeping.

Two hours later, Magda somehow single-handedly buried her brother in his apple orchard. Heinrich's friend had kept Emil occupied showing him the pigs and other farm animals. When Magda came for him, he ran to her and asked where Frederich was.

She smiled and said, "We'll see him soon."

**

CHAPTER

Port Locke, Massachusetts

After the break-in, my brother Doc brought me a little present – which he dropped noisily onto my brunch bar while staring at me intently.

"What in the hell is that?" I inquired.

"It's a gun. Uncle Slug's to be precise. Don't you remember shooting at tin cans and a few rats at the dump?"

"Vividly, and it was a disgusting experience. Why is it here, this gun?"

"I think you need it."

"I don't' want a gun, Brother Dear."

"Why not? You were a pretty good shot. Remember that V8 can that you shot right through the carrot?"

"That was a fluke."

"No, it wasn't. You could hit anything you aimed at. You did better than Uncle Slug. That's why he got pissed and took us home."

"Okay, fine. If I'm ever being chased by a V8 can, I'll borrow the gun."

"Keep it," he insisted.

"No, I'm liable to shoot the cat if I hear a noise some night."

"It's more likely that Phinney would take the gun away and shoot you."

Doc respected feline superiority and the cat appreciated it. My brother especially enjoyed when Phineas would shuffle through typed pages of my work for the paper, and finding a piece of work particularly wanting, hock a hairball on it to express his disapproval. His instincts were really quite good.

"Just take the stupid thing with you when you leave which is now because we're going to The Port-o-Call for lunch. I'm thinking *chowdah...*"

Doc replied, "No, let's go to *Glosstah fa lobstah.*" Our cousins from Connecticut loved to ridicule our accents and Doc and I had a whole shtick we did for their benefit. Doc's answer to the inevitable question DO YOU PAHK YOUR CAH IN HAHVAHD YAHD? was, "No, because it's too far to walk to Boston College."

He picked up the revolver and twirled it around his finger like a gunslinger, saying, "Hey podner, let's go someplace where I can shoot my own lobster."

"Cut that out, and don't get caught with it either, Dumdum."

He shrugged and jammed the gun into his jacket pocket. I visited the powder room, and we left for lunch.

**

CHAPTER

Session

"How can someone just be gone?" I shook my head. "She's been there since I was seven years old. She *cannot* be gone."

Doctor S. nodded and I continued.

"The world's full of people that deserve to be killed...but she didn't. I just want to know what happened. I know it won't change things, but at least whoever did it can give us a reason...even if that reason is just that they've got a screw loose. I need to know why it happened."

"You realize that murder cases aren't always solved."

I blinked and hot tears rolled down my cheeks, surprising us both.

Doctor S. pushed a flower-covered box of Kleenex toward me.

"Are you allowed to deduct these?" I asked. The taxable status of her tissues was suddenly very important to me and when she nodded in the affirmative, I patted my face and said, "Sorry. I don't usually cry."

"I know. You have panic attacks instead."

I wiped my nose and said, "Well, they're a lot less messy."

Since the funeral I had experienced a number of the DON'T LET ME DIE/PLEASE LET ME DIE debilitations. Doctor S. had asked if I wanted to try medication, but I was leery of pharmaceutical cures and I knew that unpleasant though they were, I had survived the attacks. Each time it happened I wanted to tell someone to call an ambulance or an undertaker, but fortunately, I can't speak; and then it passes.

**

CHAPTER

Port Locke, Massachusetts

"Hey, Gordo! How was your head after that Friday night?" Todd Somersworth shouted from the bar at the Widow Perkins when he saw his old friend enter the pub.

Gordo froze. *What Friday night?*

Todd was the only preppie in the world that Gordo liked. They were neighbors and had been friends since childhood.

"You were quite stinky-eyed," Todd continued as Gordo walked toward him at the bar. He laughed uncertainly, sat down next to Todd and ordered a Molson.

"Anything to be ashamed of? Not that I'm too familiar with shame."

Todd slugged down a long draft of his beer, banged the bottle on the bar and made a yummy sound.

"Nah, you were cool.

Drinkers would tell other drinkers that their behavior had been perfect if that behavior had included beheading the Christ child at a black mass.

"I drove you in your motorcar and down to Revere Beach and back so the car would know what real handler felt like."

Gordo needed more information without admitting that he didn't remember.

"I let *you* drive Black Beauty?"

Todd chuckled. "Something like that. You passed out in the passenger's seat and I took that as permission. The wind whistling through what's left of your locks woke you up somewhere on the Lynnway."

Gordo pointed out that his receding hairline only served to make him look more mature than Todd, and he'd always looked smarter. He encouraged Todd to continue.

"Then we went to my abode where you threw up in the kitty litter box and passed out again. Mr. Brillstang *(named after their high school science teacher; and everyone who had ever met both cat and teacher agreed that the resemblance was uncanny)* resented your fouling of his box. And frankly you weren't particularly good company. I was forced to sit up all night making phone calls to people I like a lot less. Like the Pope."

"You called the Pope?" Gordo was delighted.

"Yes, and I had some really good advice for him, but they refused to put me through," Todd pouted.

"Because you sound like a Protestant."

"It's more likely that even at the Vatican they could hear you snoring like a drunken hog from the floor by the litter box, where you lay until dawn's early light..."

The beer bottle stopped midway to Gordo's mouth. "Dawn's early light...I was there *all* night?"

Todd nodded in the affirmative, a cigarette dangling from his lips as he searched his pockets for a book of matches that he couldn't seem to find.

Gordo leaped up from his bar stool, took Todd by the shoulders and kissed him on both cheeks. Then he headed for the door, whistling.

Todd waved Jodie the bartender over and asked in an anxious whisper, "Do you think he'll call?"

She sighed and said, "Not if he's smart," and opened up another beer for her favorite customer.

** **

Having announced my alcoholism and perhaps an upcoming stint in a rehab for all to enjoy at Easter dinner, I was about to repair to the TV room to watch *Murder, She Wrote*. As I rose, my scandalized mother sniffed, "In my day, we didn't have…"

Trailing off, she gave me the opportunity to finish her statement.

"The habit of calling things by their proper names?" I offered.

This won no points, but if she was about to suggest there were no alcoholics in her family, I was going to personally have her committed.

My father's theory about my mother's family was that they were all borderline insane to start with, so it only took a bite of a rum cake to push them over the edge.

Most family holidays featured charred turkeys, someone picking at an emotional scab until someone else bled, fisticuffs, flying insults and ashtrays. Good Irish fun. And no one ever said a word afterward. We were never specifically told not to; it was just understood. There's a pretty clear message in silence.

Also, we were not to disrespect our elders, even when they acted like maniacs. One Thanksgiving I was reprimanded by my mother in front of a roomful of people for sneering at my aunt while she slobbered drunkenly all over her toddler grandson, crying and telling him about his parents' upcoming divorce. I was a teenager at the time and becoming rather sick of their shit. I stomped out of the room and Doc followed me.

We went out on the back porch and lit cigarettes. "It's not you, Kit. They're all crazy," he told me between drags.

"How can people do that to little kids?" I demanded to know. Doc blew out smoke and shook his head. He was upset for little Jonathan too. We knew that the kid was really too young to understand what the so-called adult was telling him, but he must have known it wasn't anything good.

My father, who could drink his little juice glasses of red wine all day without a hint of having a psychotic episode, came out to the porch and put one arm around me and the other around Doc.

"Those fools can't hold a drink and they'll never admit it," he told us. That sized things up rather well, I thought. "Come on back in." We did, but I couldn't help reflecting on how good my mother was at identifying problems in other families and how blind she was to her own.

**

I dashed into the Daily Union office suite a little late, as was my custom, and the employees who were huddled near the office entrance doors abruptly hushed. Some of the group began examining the floor tiles closely while others suddenly remembered that they were needed in another department.

The air was crackling with whatever the news was. I crossed the outer office to the elevator just as Ellie was exiting it. She looked unhappy. She took my arm, pulled me into the elevator and closed the door.

"Did you hear?" she stage-whispered.

"No, what?"

"Doyle went back to England. He left last night."

"Why? What happened?" thinking that one of the owners of the Daily Union had caught him in the wrong mood.

"His wife had a heart attack."

"Oh God...is she still with us?"

"Just barely, I guess," Ellie shook her head. "He probably won't be back for a while."

"Shit, shit, shit."

"Agreed – and I can't wait to see which pinhead they put in charge."

"Well at least we know it won't be one of us," I said and we chuckled. "Seriously, though, it should be you."

She shook her head. "You know the rules of the game, kid."

I did know the rules and they sucked.

That night I had dreams I couldn't remember, and awoke with an intense sadness and the thought *No one should have to do this* and I didn't know why.

**

CHAPTER

Bamberg, Germany

Half-mad with grief, Magda stirred crushed mint into the mixture in the wooden bowl, to cut the bitterness of the other herbs.

No one should have to do this...but what choice was there? They would come for her. Between her friendship with Anke and the wounds visited upon the prince bishop's guardsmen by her brother, it was only a question of when. Then who would care for Emil? Her neighbors could barely feed themselves and she couldn't bear to imagine the fate of the child of an executed witch in the hands of the authorities. She stirred the herb mixture into a large bowl of bread dough, bowed her head and quietly spoke a few Latin words.

**

They came on horseback. Magda listened to the distant pace of the horses' hooves and the shouts of the guards and determined that there was little time, but enough. She called to Emil and offered him a piece of warm bread. When he reached for it, she picked him up and kissed his cheek as he began to chew. She tore off a larger piece and pocketed it, and with Emil in her arms, hurried from the cottage, up the hill to Frederich's orchard.

They sat down under one of the larger apple trees near Frederich's grave. Magda put both arms around Emil as he began to drowse, then quickly chewed and swallowed her bread. Within minutes, they were both unconscious. Magda had planned it well and their hearts stopping beating at exactly the same moment.

**

The guards arrived and burst noisily into the empty cottage. Captain Brimmel, their leader, was aching and lame from an injury sustained during the brawl with Frederich. To offset his discomfort, he intended to inflict as much pain as possible on Magda before he killed her.

Brimmel noticed the bread on the table, put his hand on it and found it warm. He ordered the others to search outside, barking that she couldn't have gone far.

The guardsmen dispersed. Brimmel sat down to rest his leg and could think of no reason not to partake of the warm bread.

"She won't need it," he chuckled to himself. He tore off a huge chunk and shoved it into his mouth.

Normally, the guards who found Magda would have subjected her, dead or alive, to their pleasures; but the sight of the beautiful blonde child in her arms stilled them. They each in turn stared at the pair and then turned and trudged silently back to the cottage, where they found Brimmel slumped over the table, dead.

He had not been a popular officer, but his men respectfully carried his body outside and laid him across his horse's back. The officer who was second in command sent the youngest guard back in to search the cottage for valuables, but he found none. Turning in disgust to leave, the soldier spied what was left of the large loaf of bread on the table, and thinking that a few of them would have a bit of sustenance for the ride back to town, hid it under his cloak.

**

CHAPTER

Port Locke, Massachusetts

I was wishing that I hadn't answered the phone. I almost always wish that I hadn't answered the phone.

"Are you kidding me? Why there, of all the goddamned places in the ..."

Molly interrupted, sounding distressed. "Just *please* come over here."

"I will if you'll be so kind as to tell me why."

"I can't...it's a surprise."

"It's not my birthday," I informed her.

"Please, Kit, will you just do it?"

I was mystified. "Oh, all right, if you insist."

"I do, I do," she pleaded.

I hung up, vowing never to pick up the receiver again unless it was to order a pizza.

**

It was raining, and except for the fact that it was dark, it was reminiscent of the day that I had been avoiding the same nasty puddle areas in the same green suede boots.

Hoping it would be nothing like my last surprise at the Frig, I proceeded, with a growing revulsion. Had Molly flipped her lid completely? She had sounded weird on the phone, even for her.

What was the freakin' surprise? My telling Molly *It's not my birthday* kept circling my brain drain. Suddenly, I stopped and stamped my soggy boots three times, accompanied by "Shit, shit, shit." I had been so stupid.

**

It appeared to be dark inside the Frig. There was a CLOSED sign on the door, but it had been left slightly ajar.

"Moll?" I yelled, pushing in the door.

She answered, "In the poolroom." She sounded even stranger than she had on the phone.

I was displeased, but not all that surprised by what I found in the poolroom.

Both of Molly's hands were grasping Walt's wrist as he held the point of a very large knife under her chin. Walt's eyes were on mine, looking amused.

I didn't move. I had always tiptoed around this lunatic and it had never done any good. My heartbeat was pounding so loudly in my eardrums that it actually hurt, but I tried to sound nonchalant.

"Okay, so I'm surprised."

Molly's eyes widened in disbelief.

"I wanted you to be here when I kill your friend," he informed me cordially. "I'm leaving you for last."

It was so simple, but it had clicked in my damaged brain too late. "You killed Cass."

He snorted and nodded. A strangled sound emerged from Moll's throat that I tried to ignore, but it motivated Walt to push the tip of the knife into her flesh and to my horror, a trickle of blood appeared.

Attempting to distract him, I said, "I know you didn't always appreciate her act, but why would you want to kill her?"

The hand holding the knife relaxed a bit and he shook his head in disgust. "She just didn't know when to quit."

Although that was a pretty accurate description of Cass's behavior, he still hadn't explained why it should inspire homicide.

"What, exactly did you want her to quit?" I asked.

There were endless possible answers to that question, and since I had no better ideas for handling this psycho, I thought I should try to keep a conversation going and then just hope that Superman would somehow get away from the Kryptonite and fly in through the window.

"So the day I saw you outside of that club, you were following me. I should have realized it when you said it wasn't your birthday," I said, disgusted with myself.

He nodded, pleased with my pain. "Guess you're not as smart as you think you are."

Although he wasn't the first to suggest that I sometimes overrated my talents, he wasn't so very sharp either, for having told me that it wasn't his birthday. In Massachusetts, a driver's license is renewable on the driver's birthday.

"And you broke into my house?"

He responded with a smile and a nod.

"Why were you trying to just scare me when you were willing to kill other people?"

"Because you think you're so fucking smart and after Cass was gone, I wanted you to see your little gang disappear, one by one. To add to the fun, the stupid cops think Gordon

Wells killed his precious sweetheart so they'll probably blame him for all of this."

He paused and shook his head. Suddenly looking revolted, he added, "All of you were always *so drunk.*"

The *so drunk* remark stung in some layer of feeling I didn't know I had. Walt was getting emotional and I was pretty sure that wasn't a good thing, so I kept my mouth shut and let him talk. While he was talking, he wasn't killing anyone.

"So, what happened?" I asked.

"You know how she was. She'd leave with anyone who asked, especially when Wells wasn't around, but the one time I make a move..."

He stopped. I held my breath. Tears rolled down Molly's cheeks. In addition to my fear, my highly inappropriate thought was that *if Molly dies, Cass would be responsible for it...again.*

It wasn't easy to pretend this was a rational conversation, but I wanted it to continue. "All right, you put the moves on and she said no. Another night she would have said yes," I said, knowing that it probably wasn't true, but I thought it might soothe him.

"Yeah, well maybe, but that night things went bad real fast. She got what she deserved."

I stuck my hands in my reporter trench coat's pockets and leaned back against the wall nonchalantly.

"And Mary Bartlett? You killed her too?"

He looked confused. "Who?"

"Feather Canyon...the dancer."

"Oh, her. Yeah, I did. I knew you talked to her and she saw me there that day. And she pissed me off – pretending to be something different when she was *just a whore*."

Maybe the plate in my head happened to shift, but something snapped. Cass was dead, Molly was bleeding, crying and expecting her throat to be cut and Mary Veronica Bartlett was *just a whore*?

Absurdly, Elvis Presley's *It's Now or Never* roared through my brain and I hit the floor, pulled Uncle Slug's gun out of my raincoat pocket and fired it at what I hoped were Walt's legs and not Molly's. He yelped, doubled over in pain and dropped the knife. Molly picked up the knife, scrambled around the end of the pool table and stood beside me, trembling.

"Call the police, Molly," I shrieked, nearing hysteria. My hands were shaking so badly that I was afraid I'd drop the gun.

"*You goddamn bitch!*" Walt screamed. He tried to turn and take a step, but the pain from his profusely bleeding leg stopped him.

"Don't move, Walt. *Don't do it*," I warned.

Knowing that he couldn't walk, he put both palms on the pool table for support and lunged at me.

I fired again and unbelievably, shot him between the eyes.

**

Molly and I stayed in the poolroom waiting for the police. While she sat on the floor and sobbed, I didn't take my eyes off of Walt's motionless body that was half on, half off of the green felt table top. I had seen too many movies where there's one last surprise left in the injured bad guy.

Officer Macklin had to pry the fingers that I couldn't move off of the gun after I had been grasping it for what had felt like hours. Molly and I were taken to the hospital and sedated.

**

My family was there en masse the next morning to take me home. "Okay, so when did you put the gun in my coat pocket?" I asked my smiling archangel brother Uriel. (Maybe the Black Rose was on to something after all.)

"The day I brought it over, when you went in the bathroom. I figured you'd find it eventually."

Luckily, I hadn't had to wear the trench coat until that rainy night. I hadn't noticed the pistol's weight, because of all the crap I typically carry in Lois Lane's pockets. My key ring is almost as heavy as a gun and my makeup kit is probably heavier.

Molly wasn't badly hurt, but will always have a souvenir scar on her neck. She now has a lot of turtlenecks and a morbid fear of pool tables.

After explanations were made by Officer Macklin, I wasn't charged with killing Walt. Anyway, you'd have to be a genius to make up a story like that.

**

CHAPTER

Session

Doctor S. managed to get a copy of the psych report on Walt, wherein his evaluator described his horrific childhood suffering of physical, verbal and sexual abuse by his sadistic alcoholic father. A succession of unloving foster homes following his father's death hadn't improved his stability. Like many damaged children, he had survived by *splintering* and becoming someone else during the abuse. The multiple personality disorder that we had jokingly attributed to him was actually the case.

Cassie's murder was exactly what Walt had told me it was, but the death of Mary Bartlett was a combination of things. He had seen her talking to me, but that in itself wasn't a big threat since he was planning to kill me, too.

The evaluation suggested that the first murder caused a control valve to blow into another galaxy; one that had allowed him to function fairly normally for years. Helpless in childhood, he had killed Mary to exert power over her and would have done the same to me and Molly. The report also indicated that his fixation on Cass was his twisted version of love.

"The sad thing is that if Cass had known what he'd been through, she'd have been his friend for life," I observed. "And he made an odd career choice for someone who should've hated to be around drinkers."

"Maybe not," Doctor S. said. "The fact that he became a bartender and then a bar owner may have been his attempt to have control over the flow of liquor and the ability to shut people off when he saw fit, which he was unable to do as a child." We analyzed it until there was no more to say.

Then she skewed my world by saying, "Do you feel ready to end your therapy?"

I felt faint. "What? Hell no, I'm still *quite* insane," I assured her.

"Are you?" she asked casually, flicking imaginary lint from her skirt.

"Well, sort of."

She stared.

I stared.

Somewhere deep beneath my panic, I knew that she was right and that we had come to the end of my need for her services. It made me unhappy because I liked her and she had helped me through a terrible time when no one else could. I wanted to verbalize that but couldn't find the words.

Instead I said, "Well, I don't want to become one of those people who can't decide what to wear in the morning without asking a shrink."

She smiled and said, "I'm here if you need me again."

Part of me wanted to say *so this is just a job to you?* Even I knew it was ridiculous. Of course it was just her job. We weren't friends. I stood and extended my hand. She also stood, shook my hand and then hugged me. She said, "You'll be fine. You know what you have to do."

I laughed, "Yes. Start drinking again."

"I don't think you'll do that," she said. I nodded and turned to go.

Then she said, "Kit, wait." I looked back as she removed the beautiful water color of Clock Tower Wharf from her wall and handed it to me.

"What?"

"I want you to have it."

"Oh no...I can't," I sputtered.

"Yes, you can. Hang it in your condo...where the chickens used to be."

I wanted to cry. Fearing that I would do just that, I looked down at the painting for a minute and then back at her. Finally, I said, "Well, thank you...for everything."

I walked home, thinking that I felt lighter...almost good. I had done the right thing by going to see Doctor Starr and by staying away from the devil's brew. I was all right. Cassie's death would always be painful to remember, as would my taking of Walt's life and his intention to take Molly's.

At home I took down the blinking *Drink Budweiser* sign and replaced it with the water color that was signed in the lower right corner by *J. Starr.*

"Looks great, don't you think, Phinney?" I asked the cat. "Maybe it's *not* just a job to them?"

The cat blinked twice.

**

A few weeks later, when Molly and I could finally discuss the ordeal, we met at the Copper Kettle for lunch. I continued my quest to convince her of the cosmic connectivity of events as I believed them to be.

"I guess I'll have to officially renounce Episcatarianism," I said.

You're an idiot." She shook her head, signaling for another cup of tea. (Irish through and through.)

I asked her if she thought that maybe Walt was the reincarnation of the guard who had attacked Cass in the past. "Then," I enthused, when he was reborn, he was taught by having a cruel parent that violence was wrong. He recognized it, but was too damaged by it to recover. He was torn between being the man he had been and the one he wanted to be, hence the Walt/Alfred thing?"

I sipped from my thirty-two-ounce Diet Coke and continued, "Maybe Gordo was Frederich. Not that all of these people have to be here right now. But he cared about Cass so it all kinda makes sense, doesn't it?"

"By the way, you talked to him, right?. How did he explain his absence from the wake and funeral?"

I chewed on a large piece of ice, thinking back to my conversation with Cassie's former beau.

"He said he couldn't be there for a couple of reasons. First and foremost, he really did love her and was sick about her death. Then there was the fact that he didn't know if he had been the one who killed her, and if he had he didn't want people sympathizing with him. You're familiar with that lovely feeling of *where was I and what did I do last night* and so am I. He regrets it now that he knows the truth, but he has to live with it."

Molly chewed her bottom lip and stared at me. "If he loved her but could never commit to her, maybe it was because he was afraid of losing her like before, in the other life?"

"Maybe," I agreed. "I never thought of that."

Molly suddenly shook herself and said, "What am I saying? I don't believe this...twaddle."

"You've got a better idea then?"

"Yes," she informed me. "We're a species that got just smart enough to understand our limitations and invented gods so we wouldn't be terrified of those limitations." She nodded her head in a *so there* manner.

"I see. Did you come to that conclusion on your own or did one of your nihilistic professors come in with a hangover one day and scribble it on a blackboard?"

"It's a personal theory," she said smugly.

"Well, Sister Fishface must be spinning in her grave."

"Good...I hope so, and speaking of nihilistic professors, David and I are no more."

The plastic straw popped out of my mouth. "What? He was so great to you after the...thing."

Molly sipped her tea and said, "Oh, of course, how Irish of you. Now that I'm not with him, you always loved him?"

"No, but I've come to respect him," I said.

I had recently developed the bothersome habit of giving a rat's ass about feelings other than my own and it confused and frightened me, not to mention that it could start taking up an enormous amount of my time.

"I respect him, too, but I've been going out with someone else," Molly stated matter-of-factly.

"Gee, don't cry too long over your lost love." I waited a beat. "Oh, for chrissake, who is it?"

She smiled like the Cheshire Cat.

"Who cares...I probably don't even know him," I said and went back to my slurping.

Molly smirked and said, "Oh, you know him."

My mind buzzed for a bit. "Gordo? That's why you were asking about him?"

Molly rolled her eyes. "No thank you. If there are two people less suited to each other than Gordo and me, it would have to be Gordo and …"

"Cass!" we said simultaneously, both laughing at the truth of our little joke.

I hate having to beg for information and I said, "Molly my dear, you have exactly two seconds before I throw this very large Coke at you. Who are you talking about?"

"Your brother," she pronounced.

I was stunned. "My what…? Who…? Which one?"

"Doc," she said, blushing a little, like she never had over the professor.

Deliver me.

**

CHAPTER

Bamberg, Germany

The order of monks that took over the farms once belonging to Anke, Frederich and Magda could grow nothing. The once fertile apple trees rotted and died; the formerly rich soil produced only weeds. The monks planted grapevines for winemaking, none of which took; and the cows and goats would give no milk.

Eventually they were forced to admit defeat and abandon the property, blaming the devil and, of course, the witch.

**

CHAPTER

Port Locke, Massachusetts

When your best friend is murdered, there isn't a thing you can do about it. Nothing will bring her back and nothing you could have done would have changed it. The most you can do is find out who did it and why. Then you attempt to understand and accept it; otherwise, you'll lose your mind.

What I've come to believe about karmic law sometimes seems too convenient, too neat. Doctor Starr suggested that it was all an elaborate fantasy that my subconscious created to help me process Cass's death and my shooting Walt; that it was just a survival tool. Maybe it was.

And maybe not.

THE END

CPSIA information can be obtained at www.ICGtesting.com
Printed in the USA
LVOW05s0103180214

374050LV00007B/100/P

9 780741 499493